Colorado Lady

• • • •

Mary Langer Smith

D0449348

ACCENT
BOOKS

Accent Books™ is an imprint of David C. Cook Publishing Co.
David C. Cook Publishing Co., Elgin, Illinois 60120
David C. Cook Publishing Co., Weston, Ontario
Nova Distribution Ltd., Newton Abbot, England

COLORADO LADY
©1988 by Mary Langer Smith

Cover design by Turnbaugh & Associates
Cover Illustration by Kevin Beilfus
First Printing, 1988
Printed in the United States of America
96 95 94 93 92 7 6 5 4 3

Library of Congress Catalog Card Number 86-72145

ISBN 0-78140-523-8

*To Mary Nelson
without whose patience,
understanding, and caring
this book would never be.*

Chapter 1

Lady Ashley Ferguson fingered the light blue traveling bonnet, spinning it 'round and 'round, smoothing the ribbons. She scowled at her parent and declared, "Father, I *do* realize I am just three weeks away from becoming thirty years old." Her birthday was not her favorite topic of conversation. Dejected, she looked down from their hotel room window into the street of the raw frontier town of Durango, Colorado. "I am probably more aware of that day than you. I am also still fully aware that I must marry before then or we will not inherit Mother's money."

For the year and a half Ashley and her father, Lord Peter, had been traveling around the world, that fact had gnawed at them both. Lately, it had given her no rest, but she could never let Lord Peter know that. If he had any idea how frantic she was, he might force her to accept the marriage proposal from the widower he had arranged for her to meet here in Durango. Lord Peter could then cease looking for the Christian man she dreamed of and insisted on having for a husband.

In spite of the Durango gentleman's pious pronouncements, Ashley questioned his Christian commitment. His answers were too acceptable, and he had been overly eager to comply with the restrictions she and Lord Peter demanded of him.

The man, an investor in the mining of the area, had neither paled nor fled when he had learned he would be required to change his last name to Ferguson. Ashley, the last of the long and noble line, insisted her children carry the brave Ferguson name.

She sighed. There had to be a man somewhere in this world who loved the Lord and who would love her for herself, not for the riches and royal position their marriage would give him.

Lord Peter thumped his umbrella on the floor, demanding her undivided attention. "And, my dear . . . . " He paused until Ashley turned to face him, then fixed her with piercing blue eyes. "Without that money we shall lose the manor house, the lands in Scotland, *and* the rooms in London."

Ashley resisted the temptation to clamp her hands over her ears, her childhood way of shutting out her father's anger. She could no longer count the number of times she had listened to this tirade.

Lord Peter, his wrath full-blown, continued his preachment unabated. "We will be wiped out socially and financially. Is that what you want? Poverty for your old age, to say nothing of mine?"

For almost two years, he had reminded her daily of this impending catastrophy. But now with the time growing so short, his voice frequently held a hysterical note. "I do wish you weren't so infernally choosy. This man has money; he is respected in his business dealings and in the commu . . . "

6

"Father!" Ashley interrupted the familiar harangue. "We are not going to discuss this further. I know it distresses you that I have refused every eligible man you arranged for me to meet in England and the Colonies."

"That has certainly distressed me in the past. But it distresses me more today because so far you have also dismissed everyone we have met in America. Ashley, we are asking a great deal of a man. Giving up one's good name is a tremendous sacrifice. When we locate an acceptable gentleman who is willing, you brush him aside like a piece of annoying lint."

Beginning at her feet, Lord Peter let his eyes travel methodically the length of her until he reached her neck. Slowly, he shook his head as he inspected the auburn coil firmly anchored there. "Must you dress your hair so severely? Why don't you try looking a bit more fashionable? You could be a handsome woman if you allowed yourself to be."

Ashley flushed under his scrutiny and critical words. Turning her head away, she bit her lip to forestall the threatening tears. "I have no illusions about my looks, Father." Despite her efforts, her voice trembled ever so slightly, and she turned back to the window lest Lord Peter see the unshed tears still clinging to her long, chestnut-colored lashes.

"Men don't want to marry handsome women, Father. They want young things, rounded and petite, who flutter and coo and make them feel strong and protective. I am too tall, too thin, too old. My face is too long; I speak full sentences on topics of substance in a firm voice, and I don't apologize for letting my brains show." She stared at the wagon-rutted street and prayed she wouldn't cry.

"Now, now, Daughter." Remorse filled Lord Peter's voice, and he stepped quickly to her side, wrapping a comforting arm around her shoulders. "You're being too hard on yourself."

Having recovered from her momentary lapse in

7

emotional control, she shook off his offered sympathy. "I am being realistic," she retorted in a no-nonsense voice. "I am good with children. I can run a household, entertain with flair, manage money—including the investments—and capably tend the sick . . . . "

Lord Peter interrupted her. "Admirable and necessary as they are, unfortunately, those are not the first qualities a man looks for in a wife. If you could make yourself just a tiny bit ah . . . uh . . . "

She turned slowly to face him. "Subservient? Is that the word you're searching for? Flutter my eyelashes? Play coquettish games behind a fan? Laugh airily at inept attempts at humor?"

Lord Peter's face reddened with his growing anger, and he shouted, "Would it hurt so much to do just a bit of that?" The volume from his booming voice rattled the chimneys on the coal oil lamps in the chandelier.

She winced but held her ground. "Yes, it would. Have you any idea how ridiculous I would look and feel pretending to be a helpless female while I towered over the poor man I'm supposed to be impressing with my frailty? And what about after we're married, and he learns that I'm not a bit like that?"

"You don't have to throw your self-reliance at him all at once. Let him glimpse your abilities bit by bit and as he grows to love you, he'll begin to appreciate what a wonderful woman he was lucky enough to marry."

"The man I am likely to attract, no matter what I do, is one who wants my money and plans to keep a young mistress on the side. No, Father. Rather than endure this most humiliating of marriage situations, I would rather spend my days serving the sick and afflicted. I will not marry a non-Christian."

With savage thrusts, Ashley set her bonnet on thick auburn hair parted in the middle and drawn severely back from her face in two wings knotted at the nape of her neck. After tying the ribbons under her chin, she snatched black gloves from the dresser and began pulling them on with impatient tugs. Working her fingers into the tight leather, she glanced over at her father. His normally florid face glowed an unhealthy purple; his eyes bulged, and he paced in agitated steps around the small room.

Perhaps I've pushed him too far this time, she thought. *But it's the rest of my life we are discussing.*

"You have no idea what it's like to be poor!" Lord Peter thundered in a stentorian voice developed through years of shouting to be heard in the House of Lords.

"Neither do you!" Ashley snapped. She whirled and hurried across the room to the bed where she began to strap her valise shut. Pausing a moment, she reconsidered, removed a long dark-blue cape, and laid it on the bed before making the case ready for travel.

Like a dog worrying a rabbit lair, Lord Peter loomed over her, sniffed, then roared, "No, I've never been poor, but I've visited the less fortunate, and I know I don't want to join their ranks."

"So have I—in hospitals at closer range than you'll ever get." She grabbed her small dressing case from the bed and plunked it down with the rest of the baggage lined neatly at the door awaiting delivery to the train station.

Lord Peter followed her to the door, took her by the shoulders, and whipped her around. Daughter and father were the same height, and he looked her squarely in the eyes. "I have been extremely patient, Ashley, for longer than was wise. Now, I am saying that if you don't choose a husband from among the eligible men I have arranged for you to meet in Cheyenne, I will make the choice for you."

His look softened. "Your dear mother, rest her soul, understood you well. She knew you would never marry if she didn't apply some persuasion. Knowing she was dying, a new will was the only way left to her." Lord Peter studied Ashley's stoic face. "Doesn't it grieve you that the noble Ferguson line is doomed unless you produce an heir?"

The question angered her. "It does, Father," she answered brusquely. "It most surely does."

His jowls trembled with his frustration and through clenched teeth, he delivered the ultimatum. "But marry you will, before your birthday! And let there be no doubt in your mind about it."

Startled by the intensity of Lord Peter's delivery, Ashley blinked at his words. Though her father had been upset with her in the past when she had resisted the proposal of someone he felt suitable, he had always respected her feelings and been sympathetic.

During their three days in Durango, however, she knew he had been extremely impressed with the investor. This morning, over a private breakfast when she had refused his offer of marriage and Lord Peter learned of her decision, he had grown livid. Now, his hands dropped from her shoulders, and he stood mute before her.

Ashley dropped her eyes and stared at the variegated colors in the cheap braided rug under her feet. Once again she forced herself to swallow her rising resentment toward her mother for that wretched deathbed will five years ago which made both Lord Peter's and Ashley's inheritance conditional upon Ashley's marriage.

Clearing her throat, she finally raised her head slowly to meet her father's gaze. "Since my happiness no longer concerns you, I have one request." Inwardly fuming, she ruthlessly pushed the emotion down, knowing she would begin crying and be unable to finish her petition if she did not.

"I will consider any reasonable request." Lord Peter exhaled a long deep sigh.

Her resentment only thinly veiled, Ashley said, "Up to now, even you must admit we have met only fortune hunters and power hungry scoundrels." Though she tried, her voice rose with the declaration.

Anger returned, flushing Lord Peter's cheeks. "I will *not* admit that," he roared. "We have met some very fine men."

Ashley glared, clasped her hands together in the folds of her skirts, and leaned forward until their noses nearly touched. "Yes, Father, you are right," she retorted. "Most were also old enough to be my grandfather and in some cases, my great-grandfather."

Lord Peter flinched under her piercing look. Then, sticking his thumbs in his vest pockets, he rocked slowly back on his heels, studying her unyielding face. Never able to remain angry with his adored only daughter for long, at last, Lord Peter nodded sheepishly. "In most cases, I am forced to agree." A faint smile brushed his lips and gentled his voice. "But, Ashley, my dear, apparently you can't marry for love *and* money, so please choose the least objectionable man and have done with it."

Ashley shivered at the thought and pressed forward with her idea. "As I have said many times in the past, I believe we can find no one suitable because you insist on telling everyone the purpose of our travels. During the trip to Cheyenne, I would like us not to discuss our titles or the reasons behind our journey."

Lord Peter's jaw dropped, and his eyes popped open like she had slapped him. "Wh . . . wh . . . why, then we'll be treated just like ordinary people. Commoners!" Lord Peter spat the word. "That will never do! Absolutely never!"

"Please, Father. We will at least know if the man is attracted to me or the money."

"Why, daughter, I can't see how it will change a thing. To anyone with eyes and ears and some intelligence, it is immediately obvious we are not of the common class." The poor man looked thoroughly bewildered.

"Please," Ashley pleaded.

Her father's face hung slack and shock registered in his eyes.

"I will have to think about it. I truly will."

"That's fine. We still have some time before the train departs for Denver. I'm going for a walk." With determined steps Ashley left the room, sped down the stairs, and out into the crisp October morning.

A brisk wind, cooled by the high snows of the San Juan Mountains to the north, swept down the canyon cut by the Animas River. The wind fought its way over rust-colored rocks and hills into the nearly barren pocket that held Durango, then drove between the buildings, whipping her skirts about her ankles as she stepped out onto the hotel veranda.

Ashley looked down the street toward the train station. Slowly, she began walking in that direction while the conversation with her father echoed through her head. She would rather be poor than marry a non-Christian, deceitful, philandering, fortune hunter, but she knew Lord Peter would never stand for living in poverty if it could possibly be avoided. She knew his threats to choose her husband were not idle.

Please, Lord, Ashley prayed, *many years ago when I accepted you as my Saviour, I said I'd honor you. I have tried to serve you and be a witness for you in every way I know how. I beg you once again to show me your will for my life.*

A dust devil chose that moment to touch down. It spun through the cluster of crude board buildings, and turned the single street of the town into a choking dustbowl. A small boy appeared from nowhere and, sprinting like a frightened jackrabbit, nearly ran over her in the blinding dust. Looking for shelter from the swirling rush of dirt and wind-borne tumbleweeds, Ashley gripped her bonnet, dipped her head to shield her face from the stinging blasts of sand, and fled through the nearest doorway.

"Ooooph!"

A great rush of air escaped from the obstacle with which she collided, but the object didn't move. Rather, she found herself gaping into a black and red checked shirt unbuttoned at the throat. "Oh, my!" she gasped, took a step backward, and instinctively grabbed to straighten her bonnet knocked askew by the collision. Her parasol fell at her feet.

"Oh, my goodness. Excuse me, please." Her words rushed out in an embarrassed tumble.

"No harm done to me. You all right?" The immovable object spoke softly and politely, but there was no warmth in his tone.

She found herself looking into the roughhewn unsmiling face of a giant. He towered over her, and Ashley reveled in the unfamiliar experience of looking up to someone.

"You all right?" he asked again.

"Wh . . . why yes, thank you." She tugged her jacket back into shape while she judged him. He appeared to be in his mid- or late thirties. She had found it very difficult to tell ages in the West. This harsh country took a heavy toll on those who tried to tame it. Dark hair curled in unruly tendrils from under a grey felt plainsman's hat and brushed the collar of his shirt.

"Have I injured you in some way? In my haste to retreat from that whirling wind, I fear I took no notice of anything." Then, quickly, lest he catch her staring, Ashley shuttered her eyes demurely and smoothed nonexistent wrinkles from the skirts of her blue traveling suit while continuing her discreet inspection of the long length of him. He had broad shoulders, a firm stomach, and narrow hips. Standing in close proximity to such an appealing specimen of manhood sent her pulse rate soaring. Frightened by the sudden and unfamiliar palpitations, Ashley searched frantically for neutral ground.

She fixed her attention on the gunbelt buckled around his waist and the holstered pistol it held. "Is that the latest in Colt revolvers?" she asked. At first eager to appear somewhat knowledgeable of Western topics, she was

13

suddenly concerned with herself that she cared.

His hand drifted over the handle of the Colt .45 and his eyebrows raised slightly in surprise. Then, quickly, the surprise gathered into a deep frown. "Not the latest, but certainly the best," he answered with cold politeness.

Uncomfortable at his frosty reply, Ashley lowered her eyes and her gaze fell on the rifle he balanced in his left hand. Her eyes widened. "You carry a Winchester '76, also? Is this country that wild?"

"Sometimes." Supremely confident, he answered her with maddening condescension.

Now, Ashley, this is not the time to lose your temper. Looking away while she regained her composure, she eyed the dropped parasol. Taking a step backward, she folded her hands demurely in the folds of her skirt, looked at the fallen object, then questioningly at him.

With obvious reluctance, he bent and picked it up. "Here." Gingerly pinching the dainty sunshade between his right thumb and forefinger, he thrust it at her. "You might need this when you next attend a shootout." Sarcasm dripped through his words. "Isn't that why you two Britishers have detoured from the usual Western tour prescribed by Crofut's guide book?"

She snatched her parasol from him. "Sir, I resent your attitude. My father and I are not searching for the cheap thrills you describe. For your information, our travels through your country have been both entertaining and informative . . . until this moment."

"Lady, I've met trainfuls of English nobility taking excursions through the Wild West. Their first comment is always about my guns and their second is to question how many gunfights I have won."

She bestowed her frostiest glare, then lest she make a misstep on her way out of the building, she concentrated on the uneven step. That was when she saw the wooden handle of a Bowie knife inside the top of a knee high boot. Her head snapped up. "I find your heated reaction to my

14

innocent comments ringing hollow when you are so heavily armed. I feel justified in asking if you are planning an attack or a defense?"

A tight smile twisted his angular features, but it didn't extend to his cold green eyes. "Neither, I hope." His eyes raised from their own study of her face and narrowed to squint through the open door.

She turned to see what had distracted him and saw an imposing stagecoach behind a six-horse-hitch wheel out of the livery barn and stop across the street. Over the top of the passenger door, *Durango Overland Stage Line* in gilt letters blazed in the morning sun.

"You taking the stage?" he asked, his voice only slightly warmed.

Why was this impossible man making her business his? She wanted to tell him not to concern himself with her travel plans, but she refused to descend to his level of rudeness. Instead, she drew herself into a rigid posture and answered him with tones saved for unruly servants. "No. My father and I are traveling by train to Alamosa and then to Denver."

"Today?"

Puzzled at his continued dwelling on the topic, Ashley nodded curtly.

He shook his head. "Not today. Not the rest of the week," he said in a firm voice.

"Why not?" Shock and dismay rolled through her. "We've received no notification of a problem."

"Just came over the wire. Tracks closed by a slide. Boy left a minute ago to deliver the news to the hotel." The sparse words clicked off his tongue as though he could hardly wait to finish the message and be gone.

"Oh, dear, whatever shall we do? We absolutely *must* be on our way to Denver today."

Through eyes slitted against the bright sunlight, he studied her intently. "You could do like some of us. Take the stage north, then catch the big train to Denver."

"We can do that?"

"If you don't consider riding in a small Concord stagecoach beneath your station." The squint never relaxed as he pulled his hat more firmly on his head. "Excuse me, your ladyship." He bowed slightly in mock deference, before brushing past Ashley and out into the wind.

"Why you . . . you . . . insufferable snob!" she stormed at him as he strode briskly across the street toward the stagecoach, never once looking back.

Swallowing her anger, Ashley ignored propriety, gathered her skirts, and ran to find her father at the hotel. She burst into the lobby, thoroughly disheveled, to see the boy who had delivered the news of the track closure tucking their last valise under his arm as Lord Peter supervised.

"You know about the stagecoach?"

Lord Peter nodded, picked up the remaining case, and handed Ashley her cape. "Boy here was good enough to advise me of the alternate method of transportation and see to it that we have tickets." Looking pleased with himself, he patted his chest over the inside pocket. "Must get on to Denver, you know. Haven't any time to lose." He studied her. "Unless you've changed your mind about our friend here in Durango."

"No, Father, I haven't changed my mind."

A grunt and a slight reshuffle of the luggage reminded the Fergusons that the boy was beginning to feel the weight of his load.

"Yes, yes. We must be off," Lord Peter said as he strode briskly across the lobby and held the door open.

Ashley stepped through and led the small procession to the waiting coach. A thin, hard-muscled man about the same height as Ashley appeared from around the stage and walked to meet them. His weathered face, permanently burned to a light mahogany by wind and sun, was seamed with wrinkles. Steel-gray eyes narrowed slightly against the sun hazed over by dust. "Name's Riley." He

16

extended his hand toward Lord Peter and the two men shook briskly. "I'm the driver." Pursing his lips, he surveyed their stack of bags. "Not very thrifty with your packin' are ye. Don't know as I can get all that stuff on. It'll depend on how many folks decide to run with us."

Lord Peter waved his hand. "Don't worry. Take what you can, and we'll have the rest forwarded when the train's running again."

Riley reset his battered Stetson, unbuckled the black leather skirt that covered the boot at the rear of the stage, and began carefully stowing each bag inside. Ashley, who had read of these vehicles, stepped back to survey the huge four-wheeled Concord stagecoach. The basswood coach was painted an emerald green and a majestic oil painting of the Rocky Mountains adorned the door panel. Though years of winter storms and dust-filled summer winds had dulled the laquered woodwork, the well oiled leather of the front and rear boots told of Riley's pride in his coach. The running gear and wheels gleamed a brilliant yellow like they had just received a recent coat of paint.

Finished loading the bags, Riley walked up next to Ashley. "Don't recall seein' ye. Be ye from around these parts?"

"We have only been in Durango three days."

"Ye know anything about these wonders?" He nodded in the direction of the stage.

Ashley shook her head. "Not nearly as much as you. Please tell us about it."

Riley's face lit like a sunrise. "This here coach weighs over a ton," he began with pride ringing through his voice. "Stands more'n eight feet high, and set me and my partners back twelve hundred dollars to buy, new." He ran a hand affectionately over the painted door panel. "Most comfortable and dependable transportation west of the Mississippi." A gleam filled his eyes and a short chuckle erupted. "As ye can testify by the unreliability of that

17

wicked smokin' monster." He spat his disapproval of trains into the dust. "Them two thick leather straps ye see under the carriage is called thoroughbraces and they's five inches wide. Absorbs the shock of the road. Ye just sit inside and rock away like a babe in a cradle on wheels."

"Riley!" The shout came from a short, portly man in his early fifties who stepped off the veranda of the stage station and extended an expensive leather bag toward Riley. "Stop your palavering with that pretty woman and set my valise in the boot." He chuckled. "Unless you'd prefer I do it myself."

Riley wasn't amused by the interruption and snapped, "Jake Harmer, ye know I don't allow nobody inside that boot but me." He snatched the case and stomped off to stow it.

As Jake tipped a black narrow-brimmed hat, the sun caught a large diamond in the ring on his left hand and released a shower of sparkles. "Jake Harmer at your service, ma'am." His smile raised an iron grey, waxed mustache on a once-handsome face. As with Riley, however, years in the elements had taken their toll and deep creases cut the planes of his cheeks and forehead, pleating the corners of his dark eyes.

Lord Peter stepped to the fore. "Lo . . . " Catching his daughter's eye, he cleared his throat and started over. "Peter Ferguson, late of Scotland." The two men shook hands. "And this is my daughter, *Miss* . . . " he paused and fixed her with a firm look as he accented the word, " . . . Ashley Ferguson."

"How do you do?" Ashley responded properly and dipped a small curtsy. Father wasn't happy with this commoner arrangement, but she gave thanks that he was going along with her wishes. Why hadn't it occurred to her long ago to do away with the titles? Perhaps it was the fuss made over them at each new stop. Ashley didn't like to think she enjoyed the bowing and flattery, but obviously

18

she must have. The sad part was that their search might have ended happily months earlier if they had been willing to travel with less pomp and show. The talk of the arriving passengers swirled around her, but she remained lost in her own thoughts until Riley's shout of "Board!" brought her from her musings.

"All right with ye if Quinn rides on top this trip?" Riley asked Jake. "My regular ain't showed up and I cain't wait."

"I don't mind if he doesn't."

A slight nod from the man in the red and black checked shirt followed Jake's statement.

"All right folks," Riley hollered. "Looks like this here's our load. Since we're gonna be together for a spell, I always like to start out friends. Won't guarantee the feelin's by the end of the ride, though." He paused and, dutifully, everyone laughed.

"Now, ye inside won't be a seein' this ornery cayuse, but in case of trouble ye'll be givin' thanks for his handiwork with a gun." Riley threw the man on the veranda a fond look. "Quinn Jones works regular for Jake Harmer as his bodyguard, but he's agreed to ride shotgun for us today."

Quinn looked through Ashley as he stepped off the veranda, touched the brim of his hat, and climbed up into the driver's box. The Concord rocked with his weight, then settled quietly again.

Ashley's cheeks flushed with his dismissal of her. This wasn't a role she was used to playing, and she didn't like being ignored even by so uncouth a fellow as Quinn Jones.

"Jake Harmer's the richest man in these parts, maybe all of Colorado," Riley continued. "That's why he needs Big Ugly up there to protect him." He cackled and pointed at Quinn who sat scowling over the scene below. "Can't find the time to count all his money and owns gold mines he ain't even started t' dig. Holdin' 'em as insurance against poverty in his old age." Riley cackled again at his joke and slapped his jeans covered thigh.

Jake tipped his hat in acknowledgment and a generous smile parted his lips to reveal crooked ivory colored teeth.

"Gideon Grove. Travelin' preacher from these parts. Him and me travel way back, don't we, Gideon?"

Pastor Grove nodded solemnly. "But so far I've made far less impact on your life than you have on mine," he said in a tired voice, and rubbed the seat of his pants. Sparse locks of grey hair showed beneath the wide brim of his black hat. Dust had embedded the felt hat until the color matched the worn suit. He moved from person to person in the circle of passengers pressing only the fingertips of offered hands. The vitality had been sapped from the man leaving only a bent, withered shell functioning automatically.

"Mornin' Star's been east, tryin' to make them white scoundrels honor their treaties with the Utes. Ain't had no luck and she's headin' back to the mountains to help her tribe get moved offen their land and onto the reservation in eastern Utah," Riley announced, a note of apology in his voice.

A woman with finely chiseled features nearly hidden by the fur-trimmed hood of her dark brown cape acknowledged Riley's introduction only by meeting his eyes with an impassive stare. Her sable brown eyes then glanced at the group, and she acknowledged the passengers with the merest tilt of her head.

Riley made a wide sweep of his arm. "These folks traveling with us from Scotland is Peter Ferguson and his daughter, Ashley. Gonna show 'em some *real* country today."

Affably, Lord Peter circled the group shaking hands, while Ashley curtsied and smiled at each one in turn.

"Well, ye've all met. Time to get aboard. Just want to make one thing clear afore we start. I'm the boss of this

20

here coach. Ye do what I say, when I say it. Don't have time fer no arguments. Ye wanna be a hero and run the show, ye travel with someone else." All the good humor had gone from his voice and face as he fixed each passenger with a steely eye.

Ashley wondered who would be brave enough to argue with that look. Her gaze drifted to Quinn Jones sitting quietly on top. His rifle rested within easy reach and she noticed the strap on his holster had been flipped off and hung loose. Was there a problem these two men weren't sharing with their passengers? Slowly, trying to not attract attention in the act, she scanned the street. Only one or two hardy souls were braving the wind. Maybe the trouble lay farther along the road. Her breath caught at the thought.

"All right, folks. Let's go! Miss Ferguson . . . " Riley took her hand and steadied her as she stepped up into the red velvet upholstered interior. Selecting the corner farthest from the door and facing forward, Ashley watched each person locate a spot. Morning Star curled inconspicuously into the corner near the door on the same bench as Ashley. Jake Harmer sat between them. Gideon Grove and Lord Peter had the other bench to themselves. With only five of them, there was no need to use the backless center bench, and they spread out in uncramped comfort.

The stage rocked as Riley climbed into the driver's box. He and Quinn visited briefly in tones too low to be heard and again Ashley wondered what worried them.

"Wait!" someone shouted. "Wait! I have a ticket."

"What in tarnation?" Riley exploded.

A pudgy, middle-aged man in a brown suit and bowler hat came running down the middle of the street carrying a black satchel in front of him like a shield. "Is there room inside or do I have to ride up top?" he shouted.

"There's room inside, but I ain't gettin' offa here to put yer satchel in the boot." Riley sounded thoroughly irritated with the latecomer.

"I don't want it in the boot," the man said.

"Who be ye?"

"Morton Sterling of Durango and Denver."

"I've heard of ye. Ain't never met ye, though. Hurry up and get in, Sterling," Riley ordered.

The door swung open and, breathless from his run, the man climbed aboard. "Sorry to keep you all waiting." His words trailed off as his eyes fell on Ashley. He blanched, then gulped so that his Adam's apple bobbed above his shirt collar. "My business took a bit longer than I anticipated," he finished lamely.

"Why, Mr. Sterling this is a surprise," Ashley said containing her puzzlement at her former suitor's sudden appearance. "You made no mention that you were planning a trip when we breakfasted this morning."

"Why, uh, ah . . . " he stammered. "I only became aware of necessity for travel after that memorable meal." He ducked Ashley's curious stare and accepted the place in the corner across from Ashley and next to Lord Peter. Sitting bolt upright, he placed the satchel across his knees and clutched it as though it were a living thing, apt to leap from his lap. His pale, flabby cheeks bespoke one who seldom saw the sun, and his hands, though clasped tightly to the handle of the bag, were never still.

"Where you traveling?" Jake asked him.

"Leadville." With that one word he shifted his body, tightened his grip on the satchel, and looked determinedly out the window.

Staring at his black leather bag, it suddenly occurred to Ashley that nervous little Mr. Sterling may have just robbed the Durango bank and be taking the least obvious—or only available—method of escape. Her eyes widened at the thought. Surely, though, if he had, there would be a commotion from the bank by now.

With every logical reason she could produce, Ashley tried to calm her fears. But each time she looked at the white-knuckled fingers wrapped around the handle of

22

that satchel, her conviction grew stronger that Mr. Sterling had committed some illegal act. And to think, Lord Peter had wanted her to marry this unsavory character. She fixed her father with an icy stare. He caught her message and shrank into the seat cushion.

Chapter 2

Outside, on top of the stage, Quinn looked up and down Durango's only street. The buildings lining it were hazed into grey ghosts by the swirling dust. The street was as empty as that of an abandoned mining town after the ore played out. Those whose business demanded it had braved the dusty assault earlier. The rest waited for the usual mid-morning lull. There was nothing unusual. Still, he had that prickle crawling up the back of his neck which had never yet failed to give him advance warning of trouble.

Riley unwrapped the reins from the brake handle. Quinn watched the old driver lace the heavy lines through the thick-gloved fingers of his right hand with practiced ease that only years of experience bring. Riley released the brake and reached for the nine-foot long whip, the official badge of authority left from the days when Riley had driven for Ben Holladay's Overland Mail and Express Company.

"Ye be ready, boy?"

This wasn't the first time Quinn had ridden shotgun for the old man. In silent anticipation, he braced his feet and grabbed for a handhold on the low railing around the driver's box. Riley, cracking the whip in the air over the horses' backs, let out a bloodcurdling yell. The startled horses leaped in their collars, and the stage sprang forward with a neck-popping surge.

When the initial clatter had subsided and the stage was rolling smoothly along the road, Quinn turned to Riley. "Why do you feel such a compelling need to start like a scared jackrabbit?"

Riley looked scornfully at Quinn. "Oh, come on, boy. Ye'd complain if ye was forced to eat steak." He cracked the whip again for good measure before slipping it into the socket on the outside of the coach, still within easy reach of his left hand. Then he carefully re-laced the lines through the fingers of both hands. Finally, he said, "Truth is, folks expect to see me make a brisk getaway. Don't want to disappoint 'em."

Quinn chuckled. "Riley, there wasn't a soul on that street to witness your flying start. I have a feeling your breakneck take-offs are something *you* enjoy."

"Ain't talkin', boy." Riley looked straight ahead as though concentrating intently on the trail. "Ain't sayin' a word." But a wide grin transformed Riley's normally sour old face.

As they clattered on through the morning, the wind abated somewhat, but the sky grew noticeably darker as a thick layer of grey clouds rolled in overhead. Quinn eyed them carefully. A summer morning windstorm was no call for alarm, but this time of year it could mean trouble.

"I don't like the looks of that sky," Quinn said, turning up the collar of his faded jacket.

Riley lifted his face and sniffed the air. "Seems I smell rain aways off. Could bring an October dowsing."

"It's not rain we need to worry about and you know it.

Rain down here means snow in the high country. That's trouble. If it's heavy, that's real trouble."

"Still lookin' fer trouble 'round every corner, ain't ye, boy? Told ye time and time again, ye gotta look on the bright side of life. Thought ye'd a-larned by now. Trouble'll find ye. Ye don't have t'go a-seekin' it."

The coach rounded a turn, and Riley reached for the long whip again, cracking it above the horses' backs. The team obliged by leaping with renewed power to meet the first incline as they started to climb into the mountains.

Though he tried to ignore it, Quinn's neck still prickled, and he turned to look behind. A rooster tail of dust from the speeding coach followed them, but when the wind blew it clear, the road remained empty.

He licked wind dried lips and tasted the grit on his tongue. Turning to face forward, he froze. There, in a wide place to the side of the road waited two men. Caution narrowed his eyes as he recognized the hardcases he'd bested in a dispute during his last trip to Denver.

Sidell, mounted on a big-chested sorrel, was forty or more. The tough, muscular man showed his ugliness in a harshly lined face and cold, light eyes squinted against the wind. His hooked nose met an upturned chin even a scraggly, grizzled beard couldn't hide. A ragged scar ran down his left cheek and locked the corner of his mouth into a cruel twist.

His partner Litch, younger, shorter and heavier, sat on a nervous black stallion, barely broken. Though silent most of the time, Litch had a hair-trigger temper which he made no effort to control. His little eyes glittered like brittle balls of obsidian. Litch methodically smacked gloved fist against open palm, and Quinn remembered his earlier threat to rearrange Quinn's face.

The stage swept past the two riders, but Sidell kept his back to the road, pointing and gesturing up the hill, apparently ignoring the passing vehicle.

Quinn scratched his head and wondered if Riley was

right. Was he looking for trouble under rocks? Turning, he gave one more quick scan to the road behind. Empty! He shrugged and settled forward again. Taking a drink to wash down some of the dust, he vowed to think on other things. Sidell and Litch were as unpleasant a topic as he knew about.

He let his mind drift. *That was some lady who slammed into me earlier. Not beautiful. Not even pretty by ordinary standards.* But she had an intelligent dignity and she didn't deserve the way he'd treated her earlier. Somehow she didn't seem like the other English travelers he'd met in Denver. *Wonder what she's doing out here anyway?* He liked her eyes, blue like the gentian that grew in shaded marshy places. Wide-spaced across her long, thin nose, they held a warm innocence that touched him. There was nothing innocent about the way she used those long, red-brown lashes that matched her hair, though. Dropping the lids until the lashes smudged the natural blush of her cheeks, and all the while she straightened her suit, she'd given him a good looking over. He didn't think she'd missed a thing. Even knew about guns. Was that what had irked him?

It bothered him that he had lost his composure with her. He kept hearing a stranger uttering curt replies until he had brushed her aside and scurried away like a nervous cat. A woman had not affected him like that in years, and he had promised himself that one would not do it again.

Inside he knew it was a good thing Miss Ferguson wasn't going to be around long. He could become real attracted to her. The thought angered him. Why did he find only society women attractive? This country held only heartache and misery for such ladies and the men and children who loved them. Even many of the strongest women, bred in the West, left for a less difficult life, and sometimes, if their bodies remained, their minds failed, and they drifted away into a gentler world. He often wondered if that's what had happened to Davey.

Thinking of Davey brought Quinn from his gloom. *Come on, Quinn, think of Davey and get your mind off women and that one in particular. Miss Ferguson's out sightseeing so she'll have something to tell the Queen the next time she's at court.* She and her father hadn't mentioned any titles, but they hadn't fooled him. They carried themselves with the assurance of nobility and a lifetime of privilege. Though it had been more than thirty years since he had been a kid in the streets of London, he had not forgotten that much. He chuckled silently. He could see the Fergusons trying to survive this wilderness without their comforts. The picture of Ashley Ferguson, an apron covering her Paris gown, cooking a meal over an open campfire amused him so much that he laughed out loud.

"Well, that's better, boy. You bin a mite sour this mornin'. Makes a long trip with a mean-face fer a shotgun partner."

"Sorry, Riley. Been churning around a few things."

"Yeah, I seen them two cusses. Up to no good, but I figure seein' ye perched up here is about as good a protection as a whole regiment of cavalry."

"Don't expect much, do you?"

"Nothin' more'n ye can deliver. Don't forget, boy. I've seen ye in action."

The stage rolled on north, the road rising steadily into the high country. The majestic snow covered peaks, however, were lost in the grey, unyielding clouds which hung low and oppressive. In the late morning, the wind picked up again and blew colder than before. Quinn reached for the knee length bearskin coat tucked beside the luggage in the front boot under his feet.

Finally, in the early afternoon, Riley leaned over the side and yelled into the stage. "Way station comin' up soon. Time for the dinner break and fresh horses."

Quinn, checking down along the coach, saw a black-gloved hand pull back the leather curtain and found himself staring into those gentian blue eyes for the second time today. He knew that if he didn't look away quickly, he'd drown in them for sure. But while his brain told him he was swimming in dangerous waters, he went right on staring.

"Mr. Jones, did Mr. Riley say we were coming to a stop?" Ashley asked, her cultivated accent adding to the coolness in her voice and eyes.

Quinn ignored her icy exterior. He was having a hard time keeping a straight face through her "misters." Riley had probably never been called mister in his whole life. Actually, Quinn wasn't sure if Riley was the old man's first or last name. Nobody ever called him anything but Riley.

"He did," Quinn answered her.

"Thank you."

The curtain dropped and the spell shattered. *Quinn, you old fool, you're acting like a young buck seeing his first doe. You're not going to love a noble woman like that and watch this country destroy her and you because she loved you, too. You are not going to think about her further. You don't even know if she's a Christian,* he reminded himself firmly.

As Ashley looked away from Quinn's eyes, she felt her face flush. *You silly schoolgirl,* she lectured herself as the leather curtains darkened the interior of the stage again. *He's an unschooled gunman who delights in boorish behavior.* Still, she kept her head averted until the heat passed. It would never do for Father to see such a reaction. He would pounce on Mr. Jones and hold fast with the tenacity of a bulldog. Since Quinn Jones didn't strike her as the marrying type, Lord Peter would only succeed in embarrassing them all. Ashley forced all thought of the rugged man riding shotgun from her mind.

She relaxed once more, realizing that Riley had been

right. The rocking motion of the luxuriously appointed coach and the deep rumble of the wheels as they rolled along *was* preferable to the smoke-filled, cinder-laden railroad cars clacking over the tracks. Suddenly, she was glad for the change of plans. Leaning her head back against the hard leather backrest, she lowered her eyes, let the stage rock her, and listened to the drone of conversation between Jake, Pastor Grove, and her father. Morning Star remained silent and withdrawn, deep inside her cloak.

Morton Sterling, sitting directly across from her, had not changed positions since he turned from the rest of the passengers at the beginning of the trip. Earlier, she had judged him to be in his mid-forties with an already pronounced soft, rounded stomach. His white, unmuscled hands indicated that he, unlike the other men she had encountered in the West, obviously did nothing more physical than dip pen into ink. Even her father, pampered by servants, gave the appearance of substance and strength, his hands calloused from working with the horses he loved.

Mr. Sterling's only movement had been to take off his bowler hat and wipe the perspiration from his shiny bald head. Ignoring Ashley as though they had never met, he stared trance-like into the leather curtain. What had altered Mr. Sterling's behavior in the few hours since breakfast? she wondered. Whatever it was had badly frightened the man, frightened him until he looked physically ill.

"We're due at the way station any time," Jake said, interrupting her thoughts. "Don't get too comfortable."

Ashley opened her eyes and turned to him. "I'm only resting my eyes."

"Sure you are. That's what my old grandma used to say, sittin' in her rocking chair. Except the rest sometimes lasted three hours or more."

How dare he compare her with his old grandmother!

That really was too much. Ashley sat up straight and readjusted her bonnet. "This is my first stagecoach trip. What exactly is a way station?" she asked, keeping in check the hostility she felt.

Jake smiled benevolently upon her. "Words can't explain this particular one. Since we're nearly there, I'll let the experience speak for itself."

The stage made a wide swing and crossed the river they'd been traveling beside. The horses' hooves drummed on the heavy boards of the narrow bridge and the sound echoed like thunder through the canyon. Ashley quickly rolled up the leather curtain and buckled the leather straps that held the roll in position. There was too much to see. She'd rather be chilly than miss this wonderful country.

And then she heard it. A faint distant clamoring that turned, as they grew closer, into a high-pitched chant punctuated with whoops and yells.

"What is that we hear?" she asked Jake.

"Indians," he answered calmly.

Her eyes widened. "Indians? Real Indians? The scalping kind?" Land! She hadn't considered this sort of encounter when she boarded the coach in Durango. Recovering from her original shock, she found she was angry. "Why didn't someone tell us of this kind of danger?"

Jake looked at her with a paternal tolerance. "Just why, dear lady, did you suppose Riley needed someone to ride shotgun?"

She searched his face for some clue to his feelings, but he looked blandly at her, not a flicker of emotion altering any feature.

Buildings appeared in the distance, and the din grew louder. The stage was rapidly approaching the way station, a collection of structures built of logs. Waving blankets and baskets, several dozen Indian women clustered in front of a square, two-story house.

Dismayed, Ashley turned toward Lord Peter. "Father!" she demanded as though he could do something about the gathering.

Lord Peter's face was tallow-colored and his body rigid. "My dear, I'm every bit as concerned as you, but I'm helpless as a lamb before the slaughter." The fine, solid voice was reduced to a croaking whisper, and his hands trembled as he searched his pockets for a handkerchief to wipe away the film of perspiration shining on his forehead.

It was then she realized there had been no shooting. "Why isn't that shotgun person doing his job?" she demanded of Jake. "Why is Mr. Riley driving right into the midst of the savages?"

Jake's mirth began as a deep rumble and rolled to a full belly laugh. Tears poured down his cheeks. Even Pastor Grove smiled wanly. Morning Star and Mr. Sterling, however, didn't see the humor of the situation and remained stoic observers.

The crowd parted as the stage barreled through, and Riley pulled the team of six to a jarring halt in front of the station. There was a second of silence, then the eerie chorus of shrill, rolling wails rose again. The women leaped at the coach like starving tigers. A large woman with heavy black braids thrust an arm through the open window and shook jewelry in Ashley's face.

"Beads, pretty lady. Buy from me." She gave Ashley a wide, gap-toothed grin. "Fancy beads. You buy?"

Stunned, Ashley remained frozen, staring transfixed at the handful of brightly colored beadwork jumping before her eyes. Jake's laughter pealed over the Indian chanting and broke the trance into which Ashley had fallen. Though she couldn't find it in her to laugh, she did manage a weak smile at the round, eager face.

The stage tipped first to the left, then to the right, as the men on top climbed down from the box. Riley's voice rose above the outcry.

"Back now, women! Passengers can't buy yer stuff if ye don't let 'em out of the coach. Give us room!"

The woman's face disappeared from the window and the noise abated somewhat. Riley yanked open the door and peered in at the passengers. "Might as well know ye ain't makin' it through to food if ye' don't buy somethin'. Who's gonna be first?"

Morning Star pushed the hood of her cape back and moved forward. "I won't have any trouble," she said softly. "These women are my friends. They have come in such numbers today to meet me." Accepting Riley's ungloved hand, she stepped down to the ground and, after eagerly greeting Morning Star, the women parted to let her through.

Ashley gulped and pasted on what she hoped was a gracious smile. Riley remained to steady her, also. Clinging to the inside strap with her left hand, Ashley placed her gloved right hand in his and watched his thick work-gnarled fingers close over hers.

"Don't be afraid," he whispered. "They won't hurt ye."

Though no smile tilted his lips, the grey eyes looked warmly on her. She nodded her understanding of his instructions and stepped down into the mob waving their hands and shouting for her attention. The next several moments, before Ashley stumbled into the main room of the way station, resembled an adventure she had had in a bazaar in Calcutta. Safely inside and still slightly breathless, she paused to examine more closely her purchase of a basket and a handwoven blanket.

"You have good taste," Jake said as he walked toward her.

Ashley laughed weakly. "It's not so much a matter of taste as self-preservation. But they are rather nice, if I do say so." She turned the blanket over and examined it carefully. Just then Morning Star walked up. "Your women do lovely work," Ashley said.

33

Morning Star's mouth drew tight and she gave only a brief nod.

Startled at her response, Ashley asked, "Have I said something to offend you?"

"You are from a foreign land. You do not know that these trinkets you buy so happily spell the end to the self-reliant life of my people." A deep sadness filled Morning Star's face and voice, and though she was a reasonably young woman, her eyes looked old and tired.

Slowly, Ashley folded the blanket and tucked it inside the basket. "Will you tell me about it?"

Morning Star slid her hands into the deep pockets of her cape, and, together, she and Ashley walked to the window looking out over the forest. "It's not actually the trinkets, Miss Ferguson, but what they stand for. My mother and grandfather tell of the old days when the Ute warriors and their wives were completely self-reliant. The men hunted, and the women tended gardens to feed themselves and their families. They made the baskets and blankets from necessity and did beautiful beadwork for the joy of creating something lovely. With the coming of the trains and the miners, the demand for their artwork has increased. Now the Utes rely on what they can sell to the white tourists. With this money they buy their necessities. This has made them lazy . . . and vulnerable. When the season is poor, there is hunger in my tribe. I will remain here with them when the stagecoach leaves."

Ashley grew slightly sick over the words she had just heard. Trying to understand, she stared unseeingly at swirling snowflakes until she felt a hand on her elbow. Turning, she looked into Jake's face.

"You ladies going to eat? The storm's finally hit, and Riley's only giving us twenty minutes for dinner. Table's this way." He pointed to a long rectangular table covered with a faded red and white checked oil cloth. Battered tin cups and plates marked the places. Her father and Pastor Grove, each wearing a beaded necklace, were already seated. Mr. Sterling, looking rumpled and distraught, clutched the leather satchel tightly against his stomach and sat with his shoulders slumped and head bowed. Not eating, he ignored everyone at the table.

"This all right?" Jake asked as he stopped at the empty chair next to Mr. Sterling.

Ashley nodded and stepped aside for Jake to pull out the chair. With a flourish, he played the gentleman, and she found herself sitting beside the mussed, distraught man. "Mr. Sterling, you didn't buy anything. That is most surely the reason for their wrath and your missing buttons."

"I will not be blackmailed into buying their cheap junk, Lady Ferguson," he said in a low, bitter voice.

"Surely you could have afforded a small purchase. They are so poor."

"They only buy whiskey with their money. I am not contributing to that."

Stunned at his accusation, Ashley swallowed her retort. Maybe she didn't know what she was talking about after all. Quickly changing the subject, she said, "By the way, Mr. Sterling, Father and I have decided to keep our titles a secret for the remainder of the trip. Would you be so good as to help us?"

He showed no visible acknowledgment of her request beyond a weak nod before he shrank back into his shell.

Loathe as she was to give up her bank robber theory, Ashley was forced to admit he didn't seem capable of such a bold act.

Since Morning Star sat on the other side of the table talking with Jake, Ashley felt isolated and concentrated on the meal before her. After tasting her small serving of undercooked beans and trying to bite a cold, hard biscuit, she decided that on the matter of food she agreed with Mr. Sterling. This meal wasn't fit to eat unless one were starving.

She looked around and saw that with the exception of her father, the rest of the diners were wolfing down their midday meal. She wondered at constitutions that could digest such fare.

"You not hungry?" Jake asked her, happily shoveling in another spoonful of beans.

Ashley forced a wan smile and picked idly at the runny mass on her tin plate. "I'm afraid not."

"Too bad. Sal makes a great pot of beans." He cracked open a biscuit and soaked up the bean juice. "Can't say as much for her biscuits." He popped the dripping morsel in his mouth and smacked his lips. "Not bad when they're softened up a bit though." His plate mopped clean with the biscuit, he reached for a second helping.

Ashley took a sip of coffee. Tasting like it had been brewed in the heel of a boot, it took all her willpower not to make a face. Quickly, she set the cup down and folded her hands in her lap. So much for dinner today.

As she sat silently watching everyone else eating, suddenly, the front door flew open. The force slammed it against the wall. Two men swaggered inside. They stood in the doorway, blinking, waiting for their eyes to adjust to the dark interior, then stomped to the table, their spurs clanging on the rough wooden boards. Though no one except Ashley raised eyes to look at the two strangers, all those at the table stopped eating and seemed to draw more tightly together as the men approached.

Holding a plate of food, Quinn appeared in the doorway from the kitchen and tensed at the sight of the newcomers. Ashley saw him switch his plate to his left hand. One by one, each head raised until everyone was watching the reaction of the three men to each other.

The hate of the two recent arrivals pulsed through the room. Ashley saw it in their eyes as they glared first at Quinn and then at those seated around the table. They stood, taut, hands hovering above their gun holsters.

"Sal!" the older one with the long scar down his cheek

bellowed. "Get in here!"

A hard splinter of a woman with a melancholy face appeared through a door at the back of the main room. "Yeah?" she answered in a deep rasping voice.

"Since when do you allow Indians, especially breeds, to eat with white folks?"

Heads turned slowly until all eyes were fixed on Morning Star. Though Quinn's face revealed nothing, his eyes turned to green ice. Slowly, he walked to the table and set down his plate.

Sal strolled over and stood behind Morning Star. "Anybody who can pay the price can eat here, Sidell."

"Didn't used to be that way."

"It's always been that way."

"Then, it's time it was changed." His hands drifted closer to the pistol handles, and he widened his stance. Litch flipped off the straps holding in his revolvers and started to edge around Ashley's side of the table.

"Litch, you take one more step and it'll be a long time before you take another." Quinn's words were almost a whisper, but they seared across the room.

Time hung suspended as the three men stood waiting for someone to make the first move. Blood pounded in her temples, and Ashley realized she was holding her breath. *Dear Lord, please protect us from these madmen. I know that you're in control of everything. Right now it looks like we need a miracle.*

Then Morning Star, her face set in regal dignity, scraped her chair back. The sound was deafening. "That's all right. I was finished, anyway."

Sal placed an arm around the woman and guided her through the kitchen door, into the inner recesses of the house.

"That's better," Sidell snarled and swung a leg over the nearest chair. Litch joined him and the two men sat down at the head of the table.

In unspoken consensus, everyone at the table stood,

37

moved away into the room, and turned their backs on the pair.

"Pie in the kitchen," Sal called through the doorway.

Some accepted Sal's offer, others left without a word. Ashley, clinging to the arm of Lord Peter, stood silently against the front wall and stared in disbelief at the two men now calmly eating. Anyone entering would never have guessed that, only seconds earlier, men had threatened to shoot each other. She had come very quickly to a clear understanding of the term "wild West."

Walking through the front door, Riley shouted into the silence, "Time to load up!"

Moving in silence lest they further anger the unprincipled gunmen, Ashley and Lord Peter found their way back to the stagecoach. The Indian women had disappeared.

Out of the intruders' hearing, Ashley exclaimed, "Snow! In October!"

"Yes, ma'am. It can happen," Riley replied. "Not likely to amount to much, though. Here's some wool spreads, just in case ye do get cold." He dug around in the front boot and thrust two thick blankets at her.

The temperature had fallen considerably during their stop and Ashley, once again seated inside the coach, bundled gratefully under the warm cover. Quinn brought Pastor Grove from the house and took special pains to tuck blankets around him before disappearing back inside the station. Soon everyone was aboard but Quinn.

Riley jerked open the door. "Got another passenger. Quinn's bringin' him. Take a short minute, then we'll be off."

Ashley amused herself by watching the giant, fast falling snowflakes twisting in their convoluted paths to the ground. It was snowing hard enough now that when Quinn arrived with a small, well-wrapped boy, he was forced to brush off a considerable accumulation of snow before

38

allowing the child to climb inside.

Ashley noticed the gentle way Quinn touched the boy. Could this child be his son? The thought jarred her; she had convinced herself that Quinn Jones was not the marrying type.

The silent young boy looked quickly at the rest of the passengers, then chose to sit on the backless bench in the center of the coach. A large black dog, its short, sleek hair already heavily coated with the wet snow, nosed inside. The child reached out to encourage the animal and the dog took a step inside the coach.

Quinn laid a restraining hand on the dog's back. "Sorry, Davey," he said, "but Hiller's going to have to ride up top with me."

The boy wrapped a hand around Hiller's neck and laid his face against the dog's snout.

"Come on, Hiller," Quinn ordered. "Davey will barely manage without your company, but the rest of the passengers will be overjoyed not to have your damp body all over their feet."

Hiller turned sad brown eyes on Quinn and whimpered his distress at being forced to leave his young master. Quinn remained adamant, however, gathering Hiller in his arms and hoisting the heavy body onto the top of the coach. With the dog out of sight, Davey retreated into a dismal little heap huddled against the far side of the stage.

While they waited for Riley and Quinn to check the horses' hitch and prepare a bed for Hiller, Ashley examined the boy. He appeared to be about ten years old, but small as he was, he might be even younger. Tendrils of sandy colored hair escaped from under his fur trimmed cap. Delicately built, Davey had none of Quinn's rugged features or coloring. *Davey probably resembles his mother.* Then she wondered what sort of woman Quinn had married.

In spite of his parents, Davey was a beautiful child . . .

until Ashley looked into his vacant eyes. They sat like large blue pools of placid water, untouched by any emotion. Something was missing in this silent, handsome child. He seemed not to look at anyone, but instead looked through them. Though his body sat on the bench, his spirit had withdrawn to another place and time.

Ashley shivered as she remembered the numbers of children like this she had seen in the London hospital where she did volunteer work. Helpless to reach them, they always tore at her heart.

Jake broke the silence. "This here's Davey." The strange boy's features remained fixed—unaltered by the introduction as though he hadn't even heard it. "He's Quinn's son, sort of. We left him here to visit with Sal's boy while we've been gone."

Ashley's heart leaped and sank. "What do you mean, 'sort of'?" she asked.

"Davey's a bit different," Jake explained. "Been like that since Quinn found him wanderin' alone in the mountains a few years back. Couldn't find out about his folks, so we unofficially adopted him."

Suddenly, Lord Peter came alive. "You mean that fine gentleman who is . . . uh . . . riding . . . uh . . . shotgun is single and a family man?"

Jake chuckled. "And likely to stay that way. Been a lot of fillies try to corral him. None managed to get more'n a smile and an invitation to dinner."

"Just hasn't met the right woman, don't you think?" Lord Peter pursued.

Jake slid over to make room for Mr. Sterling. He ignored Jake's gesture, though, and sat beside Ashley.

"I am sorry to have been so rude during the early part of our trip," he began. "I've had a lot on my mind." He gave Ashley a thin smile. "If you will forgive my lapse of manners . . . ?" Mr. Sterling looked at her with the same sorrowful pleading her bassett hound used to get his way.

Returning to the conversation Mr. Sterling had interrupted, Jake said, "I don't think there's a right woman to meet. Not for Quinn."

Ashley nodded absently at Mr. Sterling and controlled any reaction to the news that Quinn Jones was not married. That fact did not surprise her. He seemed filled with the strength and independence of the mountains and as unreachable as their granite heights. She agreed with Jake's assessment of Mr. Jones. It was highly unlikely a mere woman could touch his heart. Besides it was extremely doubtful that he shared her Christian faith or that he would be willing to change his name. No, Quinn Jones was definitely not a favorable husband candidate. And if he was, she wouldn't have him, not even if he begged her.

She almost laughed aloud. It had become such a habit with both her and her father to regard every eligible man they met as a potential husband. But that they would either one consider Quinn Jones showed how desperate they were becoming.

She attempted to force his image from her mind. The harder she tried to put down her curiosity, though, the stronger her longing to know more about him grew.

"All 'board!" Riley hollered.

Mr. Sterling edged slightly closer to Ashley. "This will give us a fine opportunity to get *much* better acquainted."

I already know more about you than I care to, Ashley thought and searched frantically for a way to escape his attentions. "I have an idea," Ashley found herself saying. "I'm not apt to ever see country like this again. I'd like to ride on top if Mr. Riley and Mr. Jones wouldn't object."

Lord Peter's mouth dropped open. "Daughter, that's madness in such weather."

"Surely you aren't serious, Miss Ferguson," Mr. Sterling protested. "It is developing into a vicious storm."

"Nevertheless, I would like to try it for awhile. I can always return inside if it gets too cold." Then, before Lord

41

Peter and Mr. Sterling could dissuade her from her plan, Ashley stuck her head out the window and put her request to Riley. With some hesitation and a conference with Quinn, he finally agreed and helped her up to sit between him and Quinn.

As they traveled the steep road higher into the mountains and the temperature continued to drop, Quinn pulled out a bear skin rug from the front boot and threw it over them. Sitting next to Quinn, though he never looked at her and only spoke infrequently, Ashley found she was having the time of her life. Her spirit soared in this wild country and despite the storm, she wanted to sing.

Riding in this euphoria, it was some time before she noticed that Quinn kept turning to look behind them. "What is it?" she asked.

He didn't answer but motioned with his head toward the rear of the coach.

Pulling the hood of her cape back so she could see better, Ashley turned around. There, following at a discreet distance, and barely discernible through the swirling snow, rode Sidell and Litch, rifles resting in the crooks of their arms.

Chapter 3

In blinding intensity, the wind drove the snow against the three figures riding atop the stagecoach and shuttered the two riders from view.

"You sure you don't want to go inside?" Riley asked Ashley.

Warm and protected in the bearskin robe and her own wool cape, Ashley shook her head, happy in the experience of the first blizzard of the winter. "Though I have been in snowstorms before, they have not had this impact on me." Then it occurred to her that Riley might be hinting that he needed more room to maneuver the horses. "Unless I am in the way, I would like to remain up here."

"Ye ain't in the way." Riley looked at her from under snow-grizzled eyebrows. "No cowardly custard are ye, girl?"

Though his choice of words amused her, Ashley glowed under his praise.

"We be gettin' close to the trail to yer mine, boy. Look

43

alive now so's I don't miss it in this storm."

"Do you live just off the main road?" Ashley asked.

Quinn and Riley both chuckled.

"I'm afraid it's more than 'just off,' " Quinn said, but he did not elaborate.

Riley provided the information. "Somethin' close to fifteen ... maybe twenty miles through the roughest country the Rockies has to offer. Only a mountain goat coulda found that vein. Old Jake's three-quarters goat and an experienced mountain man. Takes both attributes to be a success at mining."

"Plus uncommon good blessings," Quinn added, as he lifted his rifle and clicked the hammer into firing position, ending for the moment any more conversation.

At his action, Ashley felt a nervous trill run through her, and Riley cast a quick look over his shoulder.

"Don't see them two hardcases behind us. Suppose they turned tail in the storm and left our trail?"

"Not likely. I suspect they're still back aways. Just can't see them."

"It's gonna be an uneasy trip with no shotgun."

"I sure hate leaving you, Riley, but we've got a big problem at the mine." Quinn shifted his weight and took out his pistol. "I have a feeling, though, I may be the reason they're shadowing the stagecoach. With me gone, you'll probably have no more trouble."

"That what ye're gearin' up fer? Think they'll take up yer trail when we go on?"

"It's a possibility I don't plan to take lightly." Quinn squinted into the storm. "You can pull up any time. Cut in the trees up ahead is where we take off."

Astonished, Ashley questioned, "You don't mean you're going to walk somewhere in this storm?"

Quinn smiled down at her. "Thanks for the concern, but we should be met shortly by Will, our mule skinner, and a train of mules on their way back to the mine from making a delivery of ore to the mill. We'll do just fine."

Riley hauled to a stop at the break in the trees, and the stage rocked to the right as Quinn stepped down. He hesitated beside the coach, one hand on the door, his eyes sweeping the timber along the road.

Riley peered as intently from his high perch. "See anythin', boy?"

"Nothing."

"That good or bad?" Riley removed the whip from its holder.

"I don't know. I thought Will might be here already, but the storm's undoubtedly held him up." Quinn yanked open the coach door. "Jake, it's time to give up your warm seat and try some fall weather."

It was Davey, however, who emerged first. Quinn steadied him, then knelt to adjust his coat and hat. Looking into the blank eyes, Quinn hugged the little boy tightly. The look of pain that flashed across Quinn's face knifed Ashley and in that moment she felt a tiny stir in her heart. It was such a small feeling, and lasted so short a time that later, when she took time to think about it, she couldn't be sure it had occurred.

Then, Jake stepped into the storm. "Don't like the looks of this. Could make the pass a trifle slippery."

"It won't last long," Quinn answered as he straightened, taking Davey by the hand. "You know how the first snow is. Quick and heavy, then days of sunny weather after." Laying his rifle inside the front boot, Quinn lifted the pacing dog to the ground. Hiller yipped his delight all over Davey, licked his face, and raced around the man and boy in tailwagging circles. Davey trotted at Quinn's side as he strode to the back of the coach. There, he unloaded their baggage from the rear boot. "Guess that does it, Riley," Quinn called out. "Thanks for the ride."

"Sure do wish Will was here with them mules. I don't relish waitin' in this mess," Jake complained as he tucked his head down and turned into the wind.

Quinn slipped his rifle sling over his shoulder and

45

carried the bags to the side of the road, stacking them under some giant evergreen trees where the snow hadn't yet sifted through.

"Hold it right there!" a harsh voice ordered.

Ashley's heart leaped into her throat as she recognized the two phantoms materializing out of the churning storm behind Quinn. The two men who had caused trouble at the way station rode with deliberate slowness toward Quinn and Davey, their guns trained on them. *Oh, dear Lord, please protect us from these cruel men.* As they closed the distance, Ashley forced herself to think calmly. What Quinn and Riley didn't need at this moment was a hysterical woman.

How did the men get in front of us? The question leaped unbidden into her mind. One side of the road dropped down a steep bank to a racing creek, and the mountain on the other side rose almost vertically to Ashley's unpracticed eye. This turn-off to Quinn's mine was the first level place she had seen in miles of climbing.

Sidell swung out of his saddle and poked his rifle in Quinn's back while Litch covered the rest of the party with his gun. Slipping a knife from somewhere under his coat, Sidell reached out and neatly separated the sling holding Quinn's gun. He snatched the rifle as it fell and threw it into the trees. Quinn's jaw muscles worked as the beautifully polished gun stock spewed up the still dry duff where it hit the ground.

Davey didn't appear to be moved by the happenings, but stood quietly at Quinn's side, a mittened hand resting on the tense, growling Hiller.

"Quiet that dog, or I'll shoot him." Sidell's voice sounded as much a snarl as Hiller's.

"Quiet, Hiller," Quinn said in a soft, but intense tone. "Keep him still, Davey."

Davey stared into Quinn's face as though reading his lips, then responded by moving closer to the dog.

Kneeling beside Hiller, Davey wrapped both arms tightly around its neck, but the dog remained taut and alert, leaning against the little boy.

"Now spread your coat, Jones," Sidell ordered. When Quinn complied, Sidell unsnapped Quinn's holster, yanked out the fine pistol, and stuffed it through his own ammunition belt.

Just as Sidell reached for the pistol, Riley leaped to his feet and raised the whip over his head.

A warning shot ripped the air. Litch's hands gripped and regripped the handles of the pistols he had trained on the coach. A gleam lit his cruel, beady eyes. He licked his lips as though tasting the joy of the kill.

"I suggest you put that whip back in the socket real careful like," Sidell warned Riley. "Unless, of course, you'd like to see your friends here turned into wolf bait." He nodded at Quinn, Davey, and Jake.

Riley slowly did as he was ordered, then eased back onto the seat next to Ashley.

She stared at the pistol trained on her. Afraid of doing something foolish that would make the two men shoot, she pleaded silently, *Oh, dear Lord. Help us. Save us.* Too frightened to form sentences, fragmented pleadings ran through her mind.

Sidell backed Quinn up until Litch, still on horseback, could cover him as well.

Ashley felt a firm grip around her waist. "Ye be all right, girl?" Riley whispered.

Ashley nodded slightly.

"Never reckoned on this happenin'." Riley apologized. "Ain't had a hold-up in years without some real good reason."

With a smug grin, Sidell stalked down to the coach and reached for the door handle. "You inside, get out!"

"Stop!" Quinn ordered. "I don't know what you think you're doing, but you're wasting your time. There's nothing of value on board. Right, Riley?"

47

"Right, boy. We ain't even carryin' a strong box. This ain't a regular run, ye know. We jest put the coach on to help the folks stranded in Durango because of the mudslide keepin' the train from runnin'."

At that moment a leather curtain flapped open, and a flushed Morton Sterling stuck his head through. "Driver, why the delay? You could have unloaded half the people in the county by . . . . " A long rifle barrel under his nose cut short the tirade.

"Like I said, everybody out," Sidell repeated, his ugly face split with a repulsive sneer.

Undaunted and managing a surprisingly firm voice. Mr. Sterling continued, "What is the meaning of this outrage? I must be in Leadville by tomorrow night."

"Get out of there now, or you'll be six feet under by that time tomorrow." Sidell leveled the rifle at Mr. Sterling and laid his forefinger on the trigger.

"Sidell, we ain't got nothin' on this coach t' rob. Stop harrassin' my passengers," Riley demanded.

Quick as a striking snake, Sidell had his gun trained on Riley. "And you, old man, shut up! I'll decide if robbin' these folks is worth our time. From what I seen back at the way station, I'd say there's plenty aboard to make our visit worthwhile." Sidell let his eyes roam slowly and deliberately over Ashley. Though she huddled under the blanket, she felt humiliated by his look.

Ashley glared straight at the ugly man, concentrating on steadying her emotions. She would not give this odious creature and his coarse, loathsome partner the satisfaction of seeing her display fear. Even though they didn't know it, she was, after all, Lady Ashley Ferguson, descended from a long line of heroes. She would do nothing here in this wild, untamed country to defame their name and honor.

Lord Peter, Gideon Grove, and Morton Sterling, clutching his satchel in a strangle grasp, filed out and stood beside Jake and Davey.

While Litch covered the passengers, Sidell walked to his horse and slipped the rifle into the saddle scabbard. He removed a large saddlebag, tossed it over his shoulder and swaggered in unhurried insolence back to the passengers.

A crooked grin contorted his already twisted face as Sidell drew his revolver from its holster. He moved in front of Lord Peter and checked him for a weapon. Finding none, he stepped to Pastor Grove, gave him a cursory glance, then halted in front of Mr. Sterling.

"Bet you got somethin', you snifflin' little squirt. Probably a lady's hat pin." Sidell gave a hard, dry laugh. "Get yer hands in the air," he ordered as he patted the quivering man's hips.

Slowly, Mr. Sterling raised his arms, the precious satchel dangling from one hand. Sidell yanked the bag out of Sterling's grasp.

A bleating cry escaped. "Please don't take my bag. Please."

Sidell hefted it a couple of times. "Must be something mighty special in this." He thrust his face into Mr. Sterling's. "What you hidin' here, little man?"

Poor Mr. Sterling's only answer was to quake more uncontrollably. Ashley felt sure she could hear his bones rattling. Sidell tried to unstrap the bag, but with gloved fingers and only one hand, he failed. Giving up in disgust, he sent the satchel tumbling into the snow. It came to rest near where his horse stood quietly. "We'll see what you're carryin' in that later. Now let's see what you got hidden on you."

A more thorough search of the little man revealed a shoulder holster holding an ivory handled derringer. Morton Sterling's face turned whiter than ever. Saliva escaped from the corners of his mouth, and his knees shook so violently that Pastor Grove reached out a steadying hand.

"That's right, Pastor. Hold the brave man up." Sidell

tossed the little gun in the air and caught it. "See what the hero carries, Litch. A woman's gun." He cackled and shoved the miniature handpiece into his pocket.

Stepping back from the passengers, Sidell pointed his gun at Riley and Ashley still sitting in the driver's box.

"All right, Riley, you and the lady get down, one at a time. Make sure you keep your hands where we can see 'em and move real slow." Sidell made threatening motions with his pistol. "Hate to mess up this nice white snow."

Ashley, frozen with fear, showed no inclination to move.

"Better do what he says, girl. Man's crazy enough to do violence." Riley crawled slowly from the box and held up a hand to help balance Ashley.

When Sidell had them all lined up, he motioned with his pistol and thrust the opened saddlebag forward. "Now open them pockets and purses and fill this bag."

Lord Peter, his fingers trembling, fumbled with the chain that held his generations old timepiece. Apparently feeling that Lord Peter wasn't moving fast enough, the outlaw prodded him in the stomach with the pistol. This only served to frighten him more and slow his attempts to unfasten the watch. Irritated with Lord Peter's slow response, Sidell jerked viciously on the watch chain. In the heavy wet snow, the unexpected act unbalanced Lord Peter and pitched him sprawling onto the ground.

"Father!" Ashley gasped, moving to help him.

"You move one step until I tell you, and I won't guarantee what Litch'll do to you," Sidell snarled at her.

She froze in mid-step and watched her father, clothes plastered with snow, slide and slip to his feet. His once elegant brocade vest hung open where the buttons had popped off.

Thoroughly cowered by the two men, each person in turn emptied his valuables into the dark recesses of the bag.

50

When Sidell came to Ashley, he didn't wait for her to remove her gold and pearl broach timepiece, but roughly snatched it off, leaving a ragged hole in her tunic.

Giving a sideways look at Litch, he gripped her face between his fingers and whipped her head around. The crisp, wind driven air failed to dilute his rank breath as he appraised Ashley.

Fighting the desire to faint, Ashley shrank from the evil gleam in his eyes and swallowed hard against her rising panic. *Father, please protect me from this evil man. Don't let me show how frightened I am.* With a regal toss of her head, she freed her face, returning cold stare for cold stare.

With a contemptuous snort, Sidell returned to the business at hand, thrusting the saddlebag at her. "All right, lady, the rings, too."

With them covered by gloves, Ashley had hoped her antique jewelry would escape notice. Instinctively, she clenched her hand into a fist and shoved it into her cape pocket.

Sidell followed the act with greedy eyes and cackled. "Didn't think I seen yer rings, did ya, girlie? Ya forgot to keep 'em covered when ya was eatin'." Wagging a thick finger at her, he sneered, "If ya don't want yer finery stole, keep it in a safe." Then, he looked slyly at Litch. "And even that don't help much." His mirthless chortle only added to the terror of those under his gun.

"Oh, please, no," Ashley found herself pleading. "They have great sentimental value. I beg you . . . " The barrel of his pistol jabbed her hard in the stomach, a reminder of his vicious, unpredictable nature.

Casting a quick look at Quinn, she found his eyes fixed on her, his face flushed with helpless frustration building inside. A man used to being in charge, Ashley could see it would take very little more abuse from Sidell to set Quinn into action. Action Ashley feared would prove fatal to Quinn or perhaps other passengers.

51

Ashley's eyes fell on Davey, his little face drawn and white against the dark outline of his cap, and pulled into a puzzled frown. His adoring eyes never left Quinn as the little boy stood unmoving, clutching the shiny black coat of the big dog guarding him. She knew if she continued to hesitate, she would endanger their lives.

Biting back the tears that threatened to spill over, Ashley quickly peeled off her glove, removed the large, marquis cut emerald and its companion, antique gold band, and dropped them into the open maw of the saddlebag. Her heart wrenched as they hit bottom and clinked faintly against other jewelry there.

Sidell scanned the passengers once more. Then, apparently satisfied that he had stripped them of all their valuables, he closed the flap on the saddlebag and tossed it over his shoulder. Strutting to his horse, he tied the bag behind the saddle. Finished, he gave the bag an affectionate stroke, then turned to Litch, "You search Jones." He nodded in Quinn's direction, then faced the group standing together in a miserable huddle. "I'll keep 'em covered."

Litch slid from his horse and stomped his way to where Quinn waited, muscles taut and hands clenched just over his pistol handle.

"Don't even think it," Sidell hissed and trained a second revolver on Quinn.

Expertly, Litch frisked Quinn, but came up empty.

Sidell shook his head and said in disgust, "Poorest man I ever seen fer lookin' so prosperous."

Litch braced his feet and repeatedly slammed his fist into the pocket of his other hand, all the while looking with longing between Quinn and Sidell.

"No, Litch, you can't pulverize him yet. We need him."

Litch's face dropped in disappointment. He started to turn, then paused and, without visible emotion, swiftly raised his arm and struck Quinn across the cheek with the back of a gloved hand.

Quinn reeled under the blow but managed to stay on his feet. "Litch," he said through gritted teeth, "didn't you learn anything from our encounter in Denver a few weeks back? Don't make yourself any more unpopular with me than you already are."

Litch, on his way back to his horse, passed near Davey and looked down into the child's innocent face. He raised an open hand as though to slap the boy.

"Don't!" Ashley cried out.

Litch paused, his hand motionless in midair, and glowered at her. "You're next when I finish with the kid," he growled in a deep rasping voice.

His eyes fixed on Quinn, Davey didn't move or make a sound under the threat. Glancing back at Quinn, Litch met a black, merciless scowl. He shrugged, and with a little smirk which said he could wait for his fun, walked on to his horse.

"Smart kid you got there, Jones," Sidell said, nodding at Davey. "Knows when to keep his mouth shut. Not like certain others." He looked with distaste at Ashley while he moved his pistols over the passengers. Motioning with his head, he bawled, "All right, everyone back inside the coach."

When Ashley walked past him, he reached out a meaty hand and hooked her arm. "All except this one here, that is."

Ashley's blood turned to ice while her eyes flashed blue fire. *Lord God in heaven, though I walk through the valley of the shadow of death, I will fear no evil. Thou art with me. Though I walk . . .* She continued to run this portion of the twenty-third psalm through her mind in an effort to dispel the mounting hysteria.

Carefully trained over the years to control her emotions, Ashley's features remained unreadable. Not a sound escaped her lips, clamped into a thin line.

Picking up Mr. Sterling's satchel, Sidell swung into the

saddle, leaned down from his horse, and grabbed a handful of Ashley's hair, yanking it from the anchoring pins and combs until long curling tendrils spilled over her shoulders and down her back. Her head forced back, she looked up at the face leering down at her. Ashley squeezed her eyes shut and felt her knees grow watery. She swayed, and Sidell jerked hard on the hair, sending fiery stabs of pain through her scalp. After a slight pause, she felt the cold metal of a rifle barrel against her temple and her eyes flew open. In spite of the tight control she held on her emotions, a terrified whimper escaped.

Out of the corner of her eye, Ashley saw Quinn make a slow deliberate move toward the knife hidden in the cuff of his boot. Unfortunately, Sidell also saw the movement and shot him a malevolent glare. "One more inch, hero, and I'll ruin this perty thing for all time."

Quinn froze.

"That's better," Sidell rasped. "Now, throw that knife as far away as you can."

Slowly Quinn straightened to a standing position, drawing the knife from his cuff as he did so. His fury obvious, he flipped the knife away into the snow. Then, unarmed and staring at the gun trained on him, Quinn took a full step toward Sidell and shook his fist.

"Hear me, and hear me well, you blood brother to a coyote," Quinn breathed in a low, cold voice, "you harm one more hair of my wife's head, and I'll see that what's left of your sorry life turns into one long string of miseries. Let go of her, now!"

Wife! Ashley blanched at the untruth and fought against showing her shock. Bless Mr. Jones for this attempt to protect her, but she couldn't let him lie for her.

"You mean you're married to that ugly thing and that dumb kid's yours?" Sidell said, contempt darkening his voice.

"Mr. Sidell," she began in a voice choked by the angle at which he held her head. "Mr. Jones is only trying to protect

54

me. We are not married."

Sidell still held Ashley prisoner by her hair where she couldn't see him or the rest of the passengers. Apparently no one, not even Lord Peter and Mr. Sterling, made an abnormal response to Mr. Jones' startling announcement because Sidell gave her long chestnut strands a hard yank and snarled, "That why you was wearin' them fancy rings? 'Cause you wasn't married to him? Won't work, lady. Man as independent as Jones, there, don't claim a woman is married to him iffn she ain't." He gave her hair another hard jerk and Ashley heard her neck pop. "You're a fine one, denyin' your own child. Whatever made ya pick such a cold fish as this, Jones? With all the money yer exposed to, you coulda found a better looker than her . . . and a better mother."

Ashley wasn't in a position to argue more about her married state. She had denied Mr. Jones's statement and it hadn't been believed. She would leave it up to the Lord to work it out, meanwhile a quiet plea for forgiveness flew from her heart.

Sidell's cruel references to Quinn and Davey, though, turned her terror into anger and she flared at him. "How dare you refer to Mr. Jones as ugly and Davey as dumb." She spat the words, making no effort to hide her contempt.

Quinn took another step toward Sidell.

Sidell's eyes shot from her to him. "Jones, stop right where you are or I'll make you a widower this instant!" He pressed the gun painfully against Ashley's temple.

His face remained a harsh wall while Quinn backed up and placed a protective hand on Davey's shoulder.

Looking down at Ashley with revulsion, Sidell let go of her hair and said, "You, Mrs. Jones, get in the coach. Don't want someone else's old woman."

Turning to the men, Sidell smiled stiffly. "All right, folks, road's a bit rough from here on." He spoke in a chatty voice, a sudden, surprising departure from his previous growl. "But we'll let you ride as far as we can before you all start walking. Riley, get back up in the box . . . real easy like. Jones, you ride beside him, but your wife rides inside for the rest of the trip."

Sidell dismounted and with a cocked pistol, herded Quinn and Davey to the coach. He poked Quinn in the back with the rifle barrel as a sadistic reminder of his helplessness. Quinn ignored it. Setting Davey on the center bench inside the coach, he glanced only briefly at Ashley, as though afraid to read her reaction to his ploy, then climbed onto the driver's box.

Raised with the belief that a display of unseemly emotion was for the commoner, Ashley's face hid her feelings, but she was most impressed with Quinn Jones's conduct. *A true gentleman,* she concluded, *even here in the wilds of Colorado and in this most distressful of circumstances. And he has protected me with his good name.* Perhaps . . .

"Now, Riley, drive, and don't make no funny turns." Sidell's hard voice growled over the storm.

"Sidell, you sidewindin' snake, I can't drive this coach without a road. That there's only a wide trail and with this snow, there's no way a-knowin' what's under it. Could be boulders the size of yer head and smaller. Even holes and tree trunks."

"Drive!"

A slap of the lines and Ashley felt the stagecoach move. Cold and frightened, none of the passengers said anything. Mr. Sterling sat, head bowed and fingers working. Ashley felt sorry for him. Whatever his transgressions, he was surely paying for them now. Only Davey seemed untouched by the events of the past few moments. Would the little boy allow her to mother him? Although torn by the deception, she knew that if he didn't, the protection offered her by Quinn would turn to her instant death.

Resolutely rejecting those thoughts, she allowed herself to grieve for the loss of her precious rings, her mother's wedding set. She looked with agonized eyes at her father and was met by his clouded stare.

The passengers jarred against each other as the coach pitched in and out of ruts and holes and jounced over rocks. It was every bit as bad as Riley had said it would be. Then, a terrible jolt, an ear-splitting crack, and the coach lurched crazily to one side. The left rear corner dropped abruptly to the ground. The passengers grasped for handholds to keep from flying out of their seats.

"Well, that cuts it!" Jake stormed. "There goes a wheel. Wonder what the boys have planned for us now?" He pulled back the leather curtain and stuck his head out.

"Get your head back inside and tie down that curtain," Sidell barked.

Under his breath, Jake grumbled his displeasure, but complied with the order.

"At least, he's letting us stay in out of the storm," Pastor Grove said. "We should be grateful for that much."

"Yes, Pastor Grove. Think of those who are being forced to remain out in the storm," Ashley said, trying to ignore the bump her head had taken. She sat in the corner which had dropped and had received a thorough shaking with the collapse of the wheel.

Lord Peter chuckled and all heads turned toward him. "It gives me some small measure of comfort to know that the two ruffians who put us in this situation are also forced to remain in the storm."

Wan smiles broke in the faces of all save Mr. Sterling. He sat rigid, his features waxen and unmoving, his eyes closed as though in a trance.

Davey's eyes stood out, huge and dark, in his ashen little face, and Ashley offered her hand to him. He clutched it, and gradually some color returned to his cheeks.

How long they sat in the body-contorting positions, Ashley could only guess. But at last, the jingling of harnesses and the squeaking of leather interrupted the silence left by the abating wind.

With unexpected suddenness, the door flew open and Sidell's ugly face leered in at them. "All right, everybody out."

Because of where she sat, Ashley was the last passenger to crawl from the tilted coach. Lord Peter clasped her hands and balanced her as she stepped out.

It had stopped snowing. The clouds were breaking up, but even without her timepiece she could tell it was late afternoon and drawing close to darkness. She glanced up quickly at the driver's box. It was empty. What had those two awful men done with Mr. Riley and Mr. Jones? Placing a protective arm around Davey, she pulled him to her and felt no resistance in the boy.

Sedately, Hiller walked up and stood next to Davey. *I imagine we make a most domestic scene,* Ashley thought and wondered at the warm flow of contentment that filtered through her.

Muffled voices drew her attention up the trail. Holding a pistol, Litch trotted on foot through the trees, urging a scrawny little man along in front of him. On horseback, Sidell rode into view in time to stop Litch, his beady eyes glittering with anticipation, as he pulled back the hammer and placed his pistol against the temple of the bowlegged little man.

"Litch, I'm gonna shoot you if you don't mind and quit threatenin' to blow holes in everyone. When I say you can shoot, shoot. But not until."

With obvious disgust, Litch spat into the snow and reluctantly lowered the barrel of his pistol to dig it into the man's back.

Everything about Litch's prisoner was the color of dust from the worn felt hat to his battered boots. Even his bearded face and eyes were a tan color. He licked nervously at cracked lips and cast bewildered eyes toward Quinn.

"I'm sorry, Will," Quinn apologized, straightening from where he and Riley knelt, examining the damage done to the stagecoach. "I had no idea they planned anything like this. Thought when they cleaned out the passengers, they'd be happy and ride off."

"They say there's a big gold strike at the Sally Forth mine," Will said. "I keep tellin' 'em, I ain't heard nothin'."

Quinn and Jake exchanged a quick glance. "Don't worry, Will," Jake said.

Litch pulled back the pistol hammer and the click echoed in the deathly stillness.

"Litch, we don't want to kill if we don't have to." Sidell's voice sounded tired. "All we want is to get these folks to the mine, get the gold, and get out."

His guns trained on the passengers huddled against the growing cold, Sidell ordered, "Everybody pick out your favorite animal and climb aboard." He pointed to a long string of small burros waiting patiently a short distance up the trail that wound through the trees. "We're heading to the mine."

"You're crazier than I gave you credit for," Quinn said. "The snow will be frozen on the trail. It's dangerous when it's dry. There isn't a man or beast that can walk it after a snow like this."

"Don't argue with me!" Sidell shouted.

"The storm's breaking up," Quinn said, ignoring Sidell's order. "If we spend the night here, we have shelter, a bit of food, and space to lie down. Once we start up the trail, it's fifteen miles of straight up and straight down, too far to travel safely in the daylight that's left. Traveling it in the dark is pure insanity and guaranteed death."

Ashley saw Sidell and Litch exchange glances. For the first time today, they looked a bit unsure, and Quinn pressed his advantage. "Keep Will as insurance for our good behavior." He paused and looked at the two bandits. Before he could continue his appeal for sanity, however, pounding hooves and squeaking saddle leather disturbed the snow-deadened forest. Hiller bristled and pulled back his lip into a snarl.

All eyes turned to see three horsemen riding up the trail. The leader, short, but powerfully built, sat taut in the saddle. He pulled to a stop and quickly surveyed the scene. "Well, well, well. Looks like we dropped in at an inconvenient time. You boys in the process of robbing the stage, or have you finished?"

Sidell and Litch glowered at the new arrivals. "None of yer business," Sidell growled.

"Then suppose we make it our business. What say, boys?" They drew abreast of each other until they formed a wall, and all three held unholstered pistols.

Chapter 4

With a look of surprise and shock, Sidell and Litch stared at the three intruders.

"I'm asking one last time," the leader of the three men said. "What are you boys up to?" His voice, tight and harsh, left no doubt as to his intentions if Sidell and Litch didn't cooperate.

Litch moved up behind Sidell and stood mute. Sidell cast a quick eye to check Litch's position, then took a couple of swaggering steps toward the strangers. "What makes you think we're up to somethin' you'd be interested in?" he challenged.

"Don't stall around with me, you cheap rustler," the stranger snapped.

Sidell bristled. "Look here, Mister High-and-Mighty, ya ain't been invited to this here party, and ya could get real cold waitin' to be included. You and yer men ride on by and pretend you didn't see nothin'."

Sidell started to raise his gun. Before he got the revolver

waist high a shot cracked, sending a spray of snow over his boot.

A thin mist of blue-grey smoke twisted away from the end of the leader's revolver. Though the expression on his face remained hidden under the low brim of his snow-covered hat, he stood in the stirrups and leaned forward over the saddle horn like a snake ready to strike.

"Now, be a good little boy and put that gun back on your prisoners," the man ordered, his voice biting with undisguised sarcasm.

Sidell's face turned a dangerous purple and his eyes bulged in their sockets. "Why ya sidewindin' snake in the grass, who do ya think yer talkin' to? You boys wander in here, saddlebags bulgin' with a load so heavy yer horses is swaybacked from the weight, shoot up the place, and call men names. Yer either brave as a knight or dumber'n a biscuit. Personally I think yer dumb biscuits." Sidell brandished his pistol at the three men and started walking toward them. "I'm gonna tell ya once more. Move out!"

Without warning the small hatchet-faced man on the left of the leader reared forward, raking spurs across his horse's ribs. The startled gelding charged headlong up the road. Dashing across the clearing, the rider brought his mount to a sliding halt so close to Sidell that the animal breathed steamy air in the stunned man's face. Shoving back a limp brimmed hat from his beard-stubbled face, the little man leveled the long barrel of an oversized pistol at Sidell. A cruel smile inched across his thick lips to reveal stained, crooked teeth. Time stopped as he slowly cocked the weapon and took careful aim at Sidell.

Like a weighted lever too heavy to hold, Sidell's pistol hand dropped until the gun barrel pointed at the ground. A bulky man, Sidell shrank under the threat of death until he seemed only a bit larger than the small gunman. The seconds ticked off as they both held the pose.

Then, Sidell cracked. "Whyn't ya do somethin' instead a-playin' cat and mouse," he shouted in a hoarse voice. "Or are ya all bluff?"

The man holding Sidell hostage stiffened at the taunt. His hand tightened on his gun.

"We don't make a habit of wanton killing," the leader said calmly from his position in the shadows of the trees. "Besides, you haven't told us what you're doing with this coach and these people."

"And I ain't a-gonna, either!"

"Oh, I think you will before we're through with you," the boss said. "Use you for a little target practice, and you'll be singing like a canary."

Sidell paled and his shoulders slumped.

The third man rode up quietly and stopped next to his impulsive companion. He was a placid contrast to the volatile man waving his cocked gun. This man was of average size with a broad, fight scarred face and a thick mat of short grey hair burring out from beneath his soft brimmed plains hat. Older than his companions, he sat relaxed, his gun still holstered, studying the scene as though watching a play. His strange, pale blue eyes roved over the passengers, not missing a thing.

Then, slowly, he pulled a blue-black pistol from its holster, twirled it around his index finger, and pointed it at Sidell. "You heard the boss. He wants to know what you boys are doin'," he said in a quiet, intense voice.

Litch, still covering Will, Quinn, and Riley, looked over at Sidell as though for a sign. Sidell, taking the measure of the third man, ignored Litch's questioning look. Left on his own, Litch hesitated, then turned his gun toward the man challenging Sidell.

"I wouldn't do that if I were you," the boss said and let loose a volley of shots. They echoed cannon-like through the silent forest. Bullets sent Sidell's hat spinning off into the trees and snow spewing over his boots.

Dear Lord God in heaven . . . The fervent prayer started

in Ashley's heart, but terror again numbed her thoughts. *Protect us, please.*

The little man stopped moving his gun and aimed it directly at Ashley. Mesmerized, she looked into the small hole at the end of the barrel and braced herself for the shot. *Lord, I need you,* was all she could manage before her mind shut off, and she stared in dumb terror at the instrument of death.

The cruel smile again curled the man's lips as he pinned her with gun and eyes. Then, apparently satisfied that he had intimidated her thoroughly, he moved the gun away from Ashley and slowly fanned it over the other passengers.

Letting out the breath she had been holding, Ashley relaxed slightly and became aware of a movement to her left. Her eyes darted to where Davey had dropped to his knees in the snow and clutched Hiller's coat.

Oh, Davey, Ashley's heart cried, *what is all this doing to you?*

Beyond being abnormally pale, the little boy's face revealed nothing. Then Ashley looked at his hands. Davey gripped the neck of the big dog with white knuckled fingers. Hiller quivered and leaned forward, teeth bared, a growl vibrating deep inside his chest. As though asking permission to attack, he rolled his eyes toward Davey. Davey shook his head and whispered in Hiller's ear. Reluctantly the dog settled back down on his haunches. He continued the deep low growl, however. It seemed to Ashley that only Davey's unintelligible murmurings kept the dog from attacking the intruders.

Never in her life had Ashley felt so helpless. *If it is not your will, Lord, that I live, please take my life and spare Davey . . . and Father . . . and Mr. Jones . . . and . . .* Unable to consider anyone being killed, Ashley concluded, *Just take me and spare the lives of all of the rest.*

Without warning Litch flicked his pistol in Ashley's direction and narrowed his pea-sized eyes. She imagined him visualizing her death, and quaking with terror, she began once more to pray. *You spared my life a moment ago and for that I give you grateful thanks. Spare our lives, Father, please. I promise to be less headstrong and a more obedient daughter.*

Her thoughts drifted from her prayer to Lord Peter and guilt washed over her. *It is all due to my selfish and stubborn nature that my father is in this terrible situation. Oh, if anything happens to him, I shall never forgive myself.*

At the sound of creaking saddle leather, Ashley jerked around. A snow blurred silhouette in the trees, the boss now moved his black horse up even with those of his two men. He fixed Sidell and Litch with a hard look and said, "You have a choice. You boys can throw in with us or we'll leave the both of you here . . . permanently." The hard, clipped delivery indicated he had listened to enough talk. "Which'll it be?"

Sidell's eyes shot to Litch. There was no mistaking his hatred. It twisted his face, narrowed his eyes, and curled his mouth until an eye tooth hooked like a fang over the weather-cracked lower lip. A look passed between the two men.

Sidell shook his head. "We cain't shoot it out with 'em, Litch," he said in the patient voice used to reason with children. "They's too many and they got the draw."

Litch spat a dark stream, staining the snow near Ashley's feet. Then he gave Sidell an almost imperceptible nod.

Sidell continued to stare at the leader of the intruders through narrowed eyes. Slowly he reached up and set his hat with the brim low, shielding his eyes from view.

Making a great show of turning his back on the man, Sidell growled, "You there, Jones," and pointed his gun at Quinn. "Unharness them horses from the stage. They's right fine animals. No sense leavin' 'em here fer the wolves when we can use 'em. Right, Litch?"

Litch, his eyes glued to Ashley, was no longer paying the slightest attention to Sidell. He kept cocking and uncocking the hammer of his pistol. His index finger slid on and off the trigger.

A rush of panic surged through Ashley. *He's angry over the arrival of those three strangers. He can't do anything to them right now so he's going to vent his anger on me.* Her mouth dried and in spite of all her efforts, her chin trembled as she imagined the bullet smashing into her. *Please, God, give me strength to die with dignity.*

Ashley watched Litch's threatening actions for what seemed like hours. Then when he did nothing, she set her mouth in a grim line and walked toward the burros and the shelter of the pine trees. *If he plans to shoot me, at least he'll have to aim at a moving target. And if I make it to the woods alive, I can hide behind a tree.*

She heard Litch crunch through the snow after her.

"Litch!" Sidell shouted. "Leave her alone! We don't want her dead yet."

From the corner of her eye, she saw Litch stop as though thinking through Sidell's words. Then, giving Ashley a disgusted look, he grabbed her arm. Repulsed by his touch, she recoiled and felt his fingers bite into her flesh.

"Sir!" Lord Peter thundered. "Take your hands off my daughter!" Shaking with rage, he took a step in Ashley's direction.

"Don't, Father!" Ashley cried. "Please don't . . . . "

"Good advice, lady," Sidell said. Walking up to Lord Peter, Sidell poked his gun in the quivering nobleman's stomach. "Yer daughter's smarter than you. Don't make no more stupid moves. Step lively toward them burros and keep yer mouth shut."

Twisting Ashley's arm hard against her back, Litch shoved her ahead of him up the trail. She winced with the pain shooting into her shoulder, then gasped as the hard end of his gun barrel stabbed the middle of her back.

Ashley's legs turned weak and she stumbled, slipping to her knees on the slick, snowy surface. Roughly, Litch jerked Ashley to her feet, sending another round of sharp pains down her arm.

"Walk!" he snarled, drilling the gun deeper into her back.

"Please, Mr. Litch," she cried. "I plan no disobedient act. Let go of my arm. You're hurting me."

His only reply was a cruel smile. Ashley looked around for help, but all she could see were guns bristling on every side. It looked less and less likely that any of the passengers would survive this encounter.

I refuse to die like a craven coward, Ashley vowed. Throwing a hard look at Litch, Ashley set her jaw, gathered up her skirts, and kicked his shin with all her strength. He yelped in surprise and pain, momentarily relaxing his grip on her wrist. She wrenched her arm free and marched over to the line of burros strung along the tree-lined trail. As she prepared to mount one, she heard a soft chuckle.

"Wait a minute, fancy lady."

Ashley glanced over at the man his companions called "boss." He removed the hat which until now had shadowed his features, allowing her an unobstructed examination of his face. She had imagined it would be cruel and twisted like the expressions of Sidell and Litch. However, the man smiled a genuine smile at her from the heights of a black stallion. He peered through iron rimmed spectacles, the thick lenses magnifying his bright blue eyes until they lent a surprised look to his round, puckish face.

Ashley wondered if this agreeable looking person could be the same man who had been shooting and making such violent threats moments before.

"Did you wish to speak to me?" she asked.

"A lowly burro is hardly suitable for such a brave lady as you. We're going to have to do something about that."

Looking over his shoulder, he called, "You!" and motioned to Quinn and Riley still standing next to the stage.

Obstinately folding their arms, the two men leaned against the stagecoach and glared their fury at the stranger.

The "boss" ignored their behavior and said in an even voice, "Like he suggested, you two unharness those stage horses and give one to the lady." His eyes traveled to Lord Peter. "Give one to the old gentleman, too. And you, big man, ride one. Can't bear the silly sight you'd make, your feet dragging the ground." Slowly raising his revolver, he took careful aim at Quinn and Riley. The two men remained unmoving. "Gentlemen, I strongly urge you to commence your task before I lose my patience. That could prove quite disasterous for one or both of you."

Considering the threat briefly, Riley and Quinn began freeing the horses from their traces. All eyes focused on the two men and no one spoke. Finally, Quinn looked up from his work and said, "Sidell, it might be well if you explained to these newly arrived gentlemen precisely what our problem is." His voice cut with the authority of a drill sergeant.

Sidell scowled at Quinn and pivoted toward the leader. Having regained his usual truculent attitude, he ignored Quinn's prompting and asked the man on the black stallion, "What do we call you?"

A look of surprise flicked over the leader's face. Then he nodded to the right. "That's George."

George nodded slightly and shifted uneasily in his saddle. Ashley noted he was the impulsive man who had ridden forward to threaten Sidell. George still sat in the saddle like it was lined with hot coals, his gun constantly fanning the group.

"Other man's Gene."

Gene gazed at the passengers with stoic disinterest, giving no sign he heard the introduction.

"I'm Oscar. That satisfy you?"

"Never heard of any of ya. Ya ain't local. Whatcha doin' up here?" Sidell asked.

The leader ignored Sidell's question and turned to Quinn. "What kind of problem do you have?"

Quinn shrugged and tilted his head in Sidell's direction. "He's the one who made himself in charge. Ask him."

Oscar's glare bored into Sidell. "Well?"

Sidell squirmed under the scrutiny and dropped his eyes. "We gotta spend the night here. Trail to the r mine's narrow and steep. Bad enough in the daylight. Too dangerous to travel in the dark."

"What's so special at the mine that you're herding a stagecoach full of people up there?" Oscar asked.

Sidell squirmed again and looked everywhere but at Oscar.

Ashley wondered the same thing. No one said a word. The silence remained unbroken save for the wind whispering through the pines and the harnesses clinking as Quinn and Riley removed them from the teams.

Slowly, Oscar brought his gun to bear on Sidell. Litch jerked the gun in his hand toward Oscar. George whipped around, and Litch faced the barrels of a shotgun.

The two men glowered at each other until Litch, with a sour look, dropped his eyes and returned his gun to the passengers.

Oscar's eyes hardened and his face twisted into a grim mask marked with cruel lines. "Thank you," he said to George. Looking far more frightening than either of his companions or Sidell and Litch, Oscar said to Sidell, "Now, Mr. . . . . I don't believe you've extended us the courtesy of introducing yourselves."

Sidell ran his tongue over pale lips. "Name's Sidell and this here's Litch," he mumbled in a low growl.

Almost instantly the smile returned to Oscar's lips and the harsh lines disappeared from his face. If one didn't notice the hard, unfeeling eyes, he looked once again like an ordinary traveler. Ashley marveled at his swift transformation.

"I thought you might be Sidell," Oscar said. "We've seen wanted posters on you two. Not a popular pair with the people in this part of Colorado. But from what we've heard, you don't normally get involved with anything as risky and complicated as this." He let his eyes sweep over the shivering passengers and the long line of burros standing placidly under the shelter of the tall pines.

"Sidell, you and Litch can't possibly control all these people. Not if the trail is as dangerous as you just said. You'll never get near that mine before they work out a plan to jump you." He paused and carefully assessed Quinn. "And if this gentleman is who I think he is, his reputation says you won't get through the night."

Quinn ignored the remark and continued to gather the harnesses, drawing out the act to incredible lengths. He inched nearer and nearer the front boot of the stagecoach, while Riley moved to the back with equal casualness. Both men kept their heads down and seemed to focus all their attention on holding the harness out of the snow.

Lowering her eyes and looking through her lashes, Ashley tried to imagine what Quinn had planned. Since he was on the side of the coach away from the bandits, she guessed he had another gun stashed somewhere. The thought made her heart leap.

Oh, Mr. Jones no! she pleaded silently. *Don't do anything so foolhardy.* But, she also recognized, he was their only hope of getting out of this mess. If only she could think of something to distract the outlaws' attention away from Mr. Jones.

Maintaining a calm exterior, Ashley considered all the frantic, insane ideas racing through her mind. She rejected each one in turn, for it endangered the life of another passenger. Whatever she did must put only her own life in jeopardy.

Oscar made a threatening jab with his gun toward Sidell. "Got to be something more here you've neglected to share with us. I'll ask you one more time . . . what's so special about the mine that you're willing to hold up a stage and consider a dangerous ride deep into the hills?"

Sidell set his mouth in a tight line and shifted heartless eyes from Oscar to Jake Harmer.

Jake's eyes widened and a film of sweat glistened over his forehead. Frightened as he was, he still stared at Sidell in unblinking silence.

"Sidell!" Oscar's voice sliced the thin air, accentuated by the click of the pistol hammer. "I've wasted all the time I intend to."

A slow smile crept over Sidell's lips, and his eyes narrowed to slits. Spreading his feet into a wide stance and adjusting his holsters with his forearms, Sidell taunted, "Shoot me, big mouth, and you'll never know what's at the mine."

"If *you* could find out, I don't think *we'll* have any trouble," Oscar retorted.

Quinn, ignoring the exchange between the two men, continued to stash the harness in the front boot. Though appearing attentive to the conversation between Oscar and Sidell, Ashley's thoughts never strayed from Quinn. *Please, Mr. Jones, don't try to be a hero. Let them have whatever it is they want. Nothing's worth your life.* And then she saw it. An undiscovered rifle still rested in the driver's box out of sight of the bandits.

She had to do something to distract the highwaymen long enough to give Mr. Jones the opportunity he needed to get the gun, and she had to do it quickly.

71

Chapter 5

Tension crackled through the air like sheet lightning. "Listen, you saddle tramp," Sidell snarled at Oscar. "Three men ta two don't make you nothin'. With them kinda odds anybody kin talk big. Ya ain't nothin. Nothin', do ya hear me! Harmer ain't gonna talk. You'll never find out about that mine lessen Litch er me decides to tell. And you'll wait 'til yer horse grows a beard fer that ta happen." Sidell stormed off toward the stagecoach where his horse waited.

On horseback, Oscar followed Sidell matching him step for step. "Sidell, I don't believe you know a thing," he jeered. "Just a big braggart who . . . . "

Ashley saw that if she didn't do something soon, both men would be at the stage.

She gulped and called, "Mr. Oscar." When he turned around, she took a step toward the forest. "We are traveling unprepared for such weather. Would it be possible for us to stand out of the snow? Perhaps under those trees where the ground is dry?" She pointed with exaggerated motions into the dense stand of snow shrouded pines and away from the stagecoach.

As though reading her mind, Quinn straightened and turned to watch her.

"I don't suppose it would hurt for you to wait there," Oscar said, temporarily putting his argument with Sidell on hold.

Ashley flashed him a wide smile. "Thank you so much, kind sir. It is so refreshing to, at last, meet a gentleman amidst such uncivilized ruffians." Lifting soaked skirts high enough to walk through the accumulating snow, she moved to Davey and took him by the hand. Turning her back on the gunmen, she began picking her way toward the dry duff. Every eye focused on her. As she neared Lord Peter, she pretended to slip. He automatically reached out a steadying hand.

"Hold it!"

Oscar's voice stabbed through Ashley. She dropped Davey's hand and whirled in time to see all the guns trained on Quinn. Only by clenching her teeth was she able to prevent a cry of fright and frustration from escaping. Quinn's arms, in the act of reaching for the rifle, were frozen in mid-air.

Oscar spurred his horse to the stagecoach, reached out and, lifting the rifle, laid it across his saddle. "I must congratulate you," he nodded at Quinn, then at Ashley. "And you, fine lady, on a nice little maneuver. Extremely well executed. Only problem you had was that I spotted the rifle when I first rode up."

Ashley, don't underestimate this man again, she warned herself. *He's a whole lot smarter than the company he's keeping.*

"And now, Sidell . . . " Oscar rode forward until he faced the surly bandit. "I want to know what's at that mine. If you don't tell me, it will be a bit more trouble, but I *will* find out." He paused and ran his finger on and off the trigger of

73

his pistol several times. "Of course, you won't be around to know that."

Sidell paled at the threat and wilted slightly. "What do I get if I tell you?" he hedged.

Oscar bestowed a deceptively gentle smile on Sidell. "You get to live, for starters. That ought to be enough, but I'm a generous man. You boys have gone to so much trouble to set this all up, if the take's good enough, we'll give you a little something for your trouble. Depending on how big the prize is, of course."

Sidell cleared his throat and started with deliberate steps toward his horse.

Oscar's mouth twisted into a cruel knot; his eyes narrowed to black slits, and his round face set like granite.

"Sidell, I have reached the limit of my tolerance for you and your man, Litch. While it would be an added comfort to have your guns to help move these people up the trail, they are far from necessary. As I see it, the only hostages we really need alive are the big man, the mine owner, and the mule skinner to take the train. Leaves one for each of us to guard. Rest of these folks are excess baggage. They . . . and you . . . can be eliminated very quickly."

Ashley's eyes widened as his words registered. Gasps of shock punched the air as the prisoners understood their fate. Morton Sterling's face drained of color. He staggered and came close to collapsing. Jake reached out and clutched the collar of Sterling's coat, keeping the terrified man upright.

"Sidell!" Oscar's voice snapped like a whip across the deepening shadows of evening. "You're fast running out of time and so are the rest of these people." He leveled Quinn's rifle at the passengers.

Sidell let his eyes slide to where Jake busied himself with Morton Sterling. "Whyn't ya ask Jake Harmer, there? He's the mine owner."

Oscar kept his smile fixed in place and turned to Jake. "I

74

seem to be getting the well known runaround, Mr. Harmer. Now, you, sir, will tell me what is going on here. Why you are traveling to your mine at gunpoint? Speak up now or I shall immediately end your days on this earth." He pulled back the hammer on his pistol and the click echoed like the crack of a rifle through the silent forest.

Gene and George rode into position on either side of Oscar and each chose a target for their first shot. Ashley and Lord Peter weren't among the first chosen to be executed. That meant they would have to watch the others die before it was their turn. The thought brought sobs to Ashley's throat but, though she ached from the effort, she kept them suppressed.

Jake looked passively into the guns trained on him. "I'm telling you nothing. You're welcome to shoot me. I'm no spring chicken, and you'll be doin' me a favor to spare me the infirmities of old age."

"Sidell!" Oscar slammed off his horse and stormed up to the bandit. Driving his gun barrel against Sidell's temple, he placed his finger firmly over the trigger of the cocked weapon.

Shrinking under the threat, Sidell muttered, "They found a big vug."

"They found a what? Speak up, man!" Oscar ordered.

"A vug." Sidell nearly choked on the words.

"What's that?"

Ashley saw a puzzled look pass between Jake and Quinn, and they both looked intently at Sidell.

Sidell came back to life. "Ain't you been around mining?" he asked, surprised.

"No, I have not been involved in mining. What's a vug?"

"It's a cave what's walls is covered with pure gold." Greed glittered in Sidell's eyes. "Heard it's the biggest one anybody's ever seed anywhere. Vugs is usually just little pockets in the rocks where the water's eat away the limestone and left the inside with a thin coat o' gold. But this here one at Harmer's mine's big as a room and the gold's thick."

Oscar's eyes took on the same hard glitter that filled Sidell's. "How do you know about this? That's not information any smart man would spread around."

"Ya don't need ta know my source. Ya asked what we was doin' herdin' this bunch to the mine. I told ya."

Oscar aimed his gun at Jake. "This story true?"

Though he paled and his lips twitched slightly, Jake stared into the muzzle of the gun and didn't say a word.

Suddenly, Oscar leaped after Davey. He jerked the little boy by the collar until he stood on his tiptoe. Oscar jammed his pistol to the boy's head. Davey's serene face froze in terror.

Quinn took a step toward Davey, but Gene drove a gun into his back.

"Mister," Oscar said to Jake, grinding the words between his teeth, "if you want this boy to live, you'll tell me right now if Sidell's story is true." He smiled innocently as he looked into Davey's fear-filled eyes.

Jake regarded Oscar steadily. "Why should I tell you anything? Once you've found what you're looking for, we're all dead anyway. And that includes Davey. You can't afford to leave witnesses. As I told you before, I'd just as soon die right now. Leaves you empty-handed and gives my soul some satisfaction."

Oscar's face slipped on its innocent mask, and he shrugged. "We're in no hurry, Harmer." He dropped Davey in a heap on the cold, wet ground, then meandered toward the forest.

Unmindful of her own safety, Ashley rushed to the little boy's side and gathered him in her arms. "It's all right, Davey," she crooned. "I won't let them hurt you."

Oscar leaned against a tree and carefully examined his gun. The passengers stood unprotected in the storm, blue and shivering with cold. Finally satisfied with the condition of his weapon, Oscar returned to the group. He strolled up to Jake and poked the gun in his stomach. "You've got until we reach Harmer City to tell us where that gold strike is. Then, we'll start shooting these people . . . one every eight hours until you decide to talk." He turned around and looked over the stunned passengers. "Sidell, let's get the prisoners bedded for the night on the dry ground under the trees. If the trail's as dangerous to travel as you say, we'll all need some rest."

The bandits held Jake and Lord Peter at gun point while Ashley and the others gathered green boughs to make beds. Gene built a small fire, and they arranged the pine branches in a circle around it. From the stagecoach, Riley brought blankets which were spread over the boughs.

Warming his hands at the fire, Riley glowered at Oscar. "I don't suppose ye've thought about what we're to eat," he grumbled.

"I haven't considered it for a fraction of a second. I'm sure this isn't the first meal you've missed in your long and checkered career." In the shadow-filled light of the flickering fire, the planes of Oscar's face became even more menacing. "Although it might be the last."

At the threat, Riley stepped back from the fire and closed his mouth.

Oscar turned and eyed the rest of the passengers who stood soberly regarding him. Apprehension filled their eyes.

"And as for you people." Oscar paused and looked squarely at Lord Peter. "Some can use the fast." His eyes trailed over Ashley and his voice gentled. "Others will just have to endure it."

He turned and walked out of the firelight. "Boys, we need to talk." Leaving the prisoners to ponder their fate, the gunmen followed Oscar.

From the shadowed forest beyond the circle of light Oscar's muted voice could be heard, in conference with the four other bandits. Though the passengers strained to hear, the voices were only a low murmur.

After a long time, the voices quieted and the shuffle of footsteps toward the fire indicated the meeting had concluded.

Sidell was the first to swagger into the light. "Pick a partner and a bed," he ordered the passengers. "Don't want no talkin' and no funny stuff. Won't ask no questions if ya do. I'll just shoot." He flourished his pistol as back-up for his words before he turned to search out his own bed.

Late in the night the fire died to coals, leaving Ashley huddling with Davey against the cold. Cautiously, she opened her eyes and sought the location of their guard. George of the nervous trigger finger slumped against a tree across the small circle from her. His head drooped until his chin rested on his chest. She was sure he slept. Now was the time for action. If only she could slip over and get the gun dangling from his relaxed hand. Carefully she slid a foot from under the blanket.

From the pallet next to her, a slight rustle sent Ashley's heart into spasms and she stiffened.

"How did they find out about that gold, Jake?" Quinn asked in a whisper.

"Beats me," Jake replied. "Only four of us knew about it, and I'd stake my life on Bud and Jenkins. Bud's planned the security at the mine too carefully to break it himself."

"And Jenkins is the best mine foreman in the business. He's seen rich veins and vugs before. If he'd been a risk, we'd have heard about it. It sure is a mystery how those two learned about the vug."

George awoke, grunted as he stared into the glow of coals. Stiffly he pushed himself to his feet and holstered his gun. Shaking his head and raking his fingers through sleep-matted hair, he staggered toward the tangle of branches left outside the circle of beds. As he tried to separate the limbs, the sound cracked through the silent night. A hollow thump was followed by a harsh exclamation.

He probably dropped a log on his foot, Ashley thought and stopped herself from being glad of the accident.

Ashley felt Quinn tense like a cat waiting to spring. She wanted to beg him not to take so great a risk, but knew he wouldn't listen if she did. Any sound from her would only destroy the element of surprise.

Moving with incredible control, Quinn slid from under the blanket.

Footsteps thudded on the pine duff covering the ground. "Time you got some sleep," Oscar said as he approached the fire. George nodded and dropped the wood on the greying coals. Brilliant orange sparks showered through the night air, then the logs caught and blazed.

Slowly Quinn relaxed and re-adjusted the covers. He turned and, in the renewed light from the fire, his eyes met Ashley's. "I'm sorry." He mouthed the mild words to her, but stronger thoughts flashed in his eyes.

"Me, too," she answered in like manner and smiled a tired smile at him.

Quinn returned a shy grin which warmed her as much as the revived fire. Then, strangely comforted by his strength and nearness, she drifted into a deep sleep.

Chapter 6

An owl hooted overhead and the mournful sound shocked Ashley awake. Only her eyes moved, however, for even in sleep she had forgotten neither where she was nor the guns that kept her there. It had taken hours to fall asleep and now scratchy eyes and aching muscles served as a reminder that she was far from rested.

The owl hooted again, and she looked up to discover the source of the call. A big, pale-bellied bird glided silently above her on the cool air of early morning.

Shifting her gaze, she found Quinn watching her. His face was grey with exhaustion and a frown creased his brow. She opened her mouth to speak, but he laid a warning finger over his lips.

"You all right?" He mouthed the words.

She wasn't, but complaints were the last thing he needed to hear. "I'm fine," she whispered.

"How's Davey?" Quinn asked in an almost inaudible whisper.

Davey's back was to them both so there was no way to see his face without moving more than seemed wise. His breathing was regular and deep, however. "Looks like he's asleep," Ashley said.

"Something we can be grateful for." Quinn stretched and let his eyes drift to the big bird swooping above them. "It's high, handsome country where one travels so he can hear the owls hoot," he said softly and took in several deep breaths of crisp, tangy air. The air seemed to revitalize Quinn. His normal ruddy tan gradually replaced the unhealthy grey, and his brow relaxed into a smooth plane. Once more he turned to her.

"Today as we ride, don't keep your eyes on the trail. Let the horses—and the Lord—do the worrying. Gather your faith and enjoy the magnificence of God's handiwork. If you don't, you'll miss the beauty and see only the pitfalls into which you might drop. And we can't do anything right now about the mess we're in."

Ashley stared in amazement at the soft-spoken man. Never would she have suspected such words to come from one so obviously a part of the rugged western life; a man whose abilities with gun and fist were respected by even such toughs as now kept them prisoner.

Ashley did recognize his attempt to make her feel better and was grateful for the thoughtfulness. "I'll try to take your advice," she said.

His eyes darted away from her and didn't return. He looked decidedly uncomfortable as he studied the now empty sky. Finally, he said, "I must apologize for suddenly making you a wife without your consent. But as you can see, a single woman, regardless of her background, isn't safe in these circumstances."

"Even though I was dismayed that you felt an untruth to be necessary, I can't thank you enough for your concern and quick thinking. It was, apparently, your words that changed Mr. Sidell's mind. Besides, that lets me mother Davey, and he touches my—"

81

A bullet sang into the dirt above Ashley's head, and they both jumped. Her cry of alarm pierced the quiet of the camp.

"Next one will find its mark," Oscar hissed, "if you two talk again without permission." He aimed his revolvers, one at Quinn and one at Ashley.

Quinn threw back the blanket and leaped to his feet. "Oscar . . . " he began.

The low, intense sound of his voice made the tiny hairs on the back of Ashley's neck stand up. This was not a man with whom to trifle.

Quinn drew himself to full height, towering over Oscar. "You pull a trick like that again, and gun or no gun, you'll eat my fist." His big, square-fingered hands clenched and unclenched with building anger.

Ashley rose on shaky knees and went to stand with him. "Please . . . " she pleaded softly.

Quinn placed a possessive arm around her shoulders. "This lady is an innocent bystander," he said. "A victim of your greed. She has done nothing to warrant such treatment."

Oscar brandished his cocked pistols. "She was talking with you, and that's cause enough."

"She's English nobility, you back country illiterate, and she doesn't go about planning shoot-outs with yellow dog outlaws."

In Ashley's eyes Quinn stood calm and majestic, like a king. He fairly radiated strength to her, and it filled her with courage. *Oh my, but I could love this man,* Ashley thought. *Love him well and long.* Drawing herself to her full height, she, too, glared down in hostile grandeur at Oscar.

"She's your wife, Jones. That makes her suspect."

With haughty disregard for the threats, Quinn turned his back on Oscar. "I am deeply sorry about the fright caused you by this trigger happy coward, my dear," he said as he held her to him.

His touch sent little waves of pleasure rippling through Ashley. The feel of his arm, the strength he imparted, all made her feel she had come to the end of her search. *This is ridiculous,* she told herself, knowing full well she should pull away. *Here we are, held at gunpoint by these ruffians, and I'm falling in love with this wonderful stranger.*

Though her good sense told her she should, Ashley made no move to step out of Quinn's arm until she looked at Oscar's face. It had begun its frightening transformation, turning into the twisted mask that foreshadowed another violent act.

Quickly, she moved from Quinn's side. Quinn looked at Oscar and stiffened. Automatically his hand moved toward his gun. As the remembrance of the empty holster registered, Quinn looked at Ashley with stricken eyes.

Ashley's stomach tightened. "That's quite all right, Mr. Jones," she said, her voice a little shaky. "Though I am unaccustomed to being shot at, particularly before breakfast, I do consider the source of the inconvenience. Recognizing Mr. Oscar's inability to handle situations without excessive force, I must forgive him his lack."

She bestowed a slight smile on Oscar as she took another step away from Quinn. Oscar's eyes never left her. If she could only hold his attention until he calmed down.

She folded her hands demurely in the folds of her skirts, and said, "Mr. Oscar, I have not the slightest desire to be ventilated by your pistols because you think I am plotting with Mr. Jones behind your back." She tried to make her voice soothing and her words reassuring. "Therefore, I would like your permission to discuss with him the country through which we will be riding.

"What he has not told you is that I have only *very* recently come to this area. My father and I are strangers to your land. Though we have heard about its grandeur, we are still unprepared for what we have encountered."

Looking slightly abashed, the bandit scratched his chin

and surveyed the passengers all up and standing before him. "All right," he said at last, "but I want your conversation loud enough so I can hear it." Oscar's voice was overly booming. He waved his revolvers at Quinn, then made some threatening jabs at the rest of the watching passengers.

Turning, Ashley smiled at Quinn. "Is that arrangement agreeable with you, Mr. Jones?" she asked.

"It's a step in the right direction, at least," Quinn acknowledged, but now he regarded her with opaque eyes, shuttered and unreadable.

Confusion over his sudden coldness churned within Ashley. She dropped her eyes to shield her bewilderment from him. They both remained motionless waiting for Oscar to decide the next step.

The other bandits, looking unraveled from lack of sleep, joined Oscar and trained their guns on the prisoners.

George stomped over and paced in front of the passengers like a cocky little sergeant inspecting his troops. He gave Lord Peter's unbuttoned vest a flip, twisted Mr. Sterling's tie tight against his throat, and poked his gun barrel into Pastor Gideon's stomach. Though each man endured the insulting gestures with admirable self-control, anger glittered in their eyes.

Ashley watched the muscles in Quinn's jaw begin to work. Surely he wouldn't attempt anything at this moment, she fretted.

Just when it looked like Quinn was about to explode, the unexpected rustle of pine boughs drew everyone's attention. Davey rolled over and sat up. One hand rubbed the sleep from his eyes, the other clutched Hiller's neck.

Davey looked about until he saw the line of hostages. Confusion twisted his features, and he held out his arms to Quinn.

Disregarding his own safety, Quinn moved in long, quick strides toward the frightened little boy.

"Where do you think you're going?" Oscar's voice whipped across the silence. He darted toward Davey and Quinn.

"To get my boy," Quinn snapped. "Come on, Davey. It's all right. No one's going to hurt you."

Thus reassured, Davey threw back the cover and rushed into Quinn's waiting embrace.

Something in the scene touched Oscar. Almost instantly his face softened to its pleasant look, and he stopped short. He watched Quinn straighten Davey's clothes and rake his fingers through the tousled curls in an effort to coax the tangles from them. Then, Oscar shifted his gaze and made a great pretense of studying the dawn streaked sky. "Though it's barely light," he said at last, "since everyone's awake and up, we might as well get started to the mine."

"Yeah," Sidell growled. "I wanna clean out that vug today. Take my share of the gold and vamoose."

Not replying, Oscar strode to the waiting horses, thrust the reins to a large coach horse at Ashley, and unceremoniously boosted her onto its broad, unsaddled back. Though he did not speak, the look he gave her said volumes. Oscar did not like her. In aligning herself with Quinn as she had, she had ensured Oscar's animosity.

Quinn concentrated all his attention on Davey. He sat the little boy on a small pack burro at the front of the line and instructed Hiller to heel in behind.

Feeling she had nothing to lose, Ashley said, "Mr. Oscar." Her voice remained cool and firm. Thank heaven she had managed so far to conceal the turmoil churning inside. "Do you suppose it would be possible for us to have our baggage?"

Oscar stood next to Ashley's horse. He looked up at her and wrinkled his nose with distaste. He seemed to ponder her words as he studied the long line of burros. "I don't see why not," he said finally. "Got plenty of room to haul the stuff. Jones, you and Riley give Will a hand with the bags. He can stow them in the pack boxes." Without another glance at her, Oscar walked down the line to oversee the loading.

"Thank you so much," Ashley said sweetly to his retreating back. She noticed Sidell, without looking in it, threw Mr. Sterling's satchel down with the rest of the bags. Relief spread over Morton Sterling's countenance as the black bag disappeared into a pack box.

With the baggage stored, Quinn came to where Ashley sat, waiting. He pulled his hat low over his eyes and asked, "You know how to ride?"

She looked into the mask Quinn had made of his face. Her throat closed over the disappointment, and she gave only a quick nod.

"Jones!" Oscar shouted. "I can't hear what you and the missus are saying. Next time, I won't warn you, I'll shoot one of you." He walked swiftly back to where Ashley sat and peered intently up at her. "Probably plug her, seeing how she's of little use."

At his words, Ashley paled. Quinn's hand rested on her arm and she clasped it. He gave her hand a reassuring squeeze, then turned, and mounted a horse up the line from Ashley.

Her pulse accelerated and she looked down at the hand Quinn had just touched, expecting to see it different, somehow. Then, because she knew she was not an impulsive person, given to letting her emotions run away, she told herself she was just unsettled by the sudden turn of events.

The feel of his hand, real and warm; the strength he imparted; his counsel to lift her eyes to the glories of God's handiwork; all these things countered any argument for sanity she presented, though. Her pounding pulse betrayed her rationalizations. He was the man she had come two-thirds of the way around the world to find. Even if her head wouldn't accept the fact, her heart knew it.

86

Oscar led the procession along a path which wound its way through rocky spires and thick forests to the rim above a deep gorge. Numbed from the unaccustomed emotional turmoil, Ashley rode for a time in a stupor. On one side the mountain rose sheer and steep. On the other, the edge dropped more than a hundred feet to a churning river in the bottom of the canyon.

Then, the trail, carved from the side of the cliff, became increasingly narrow. It was barely wide enough for the animals. Fright jarred Ashley from her lethargy.

Oscar's horse balked at the sight of the narrower trail, nothing more than a ledge hacked in the side of the grey rock. He tried to rein his mount onto the trail, but the animal looked over the side, snorted, and rolled its eyes. For the first time, Oscar didn't look quite so confident. He stood up in the stirrups and looked back over the line.

Sidell sneered, "You scared to lead out?" Sidell's surly confidence had returned and it showed in his voice. "Let me take over."

Will cut in. "He's right, Oscar. Once you start on this trail, yer committed to the end. They's no way to turn around."

Oscar frowned his displeasure at the comments, then lightly touched his spurs to the big chestnut coach horse he had chosen to replace his own exhausted black. A quiver ran through the horse, and he shied slightly. At last, however, under Oscar's urging, he stepped onto the path. As he rode, Oscar watched over his shoulder as the prisoners and outlaws urged their animals onto the narrow path behind him.

Nervous at first, Ashley's horse steadied and moved without a misstep on the narrow path. As the horse relaxed, so did she . . . enough to ponder Quinn Jones. She had the feeling that had he not been encumbered by his fellow captives, he could have single-handedly sent the whole lot of highwaymen packing.

She realized that he played the role of her husband only

sincerely enough to preserve the facade and keep her safe. He played it so well, however, that a difficult tug-of-war drew her conscience and convictions into conflict with her gratitude—and growing feelings for one Quinn Jones.

The cautious, plodding steps of the animals matched her mood. Preoccupied with Quinn and her unexpected emotional response to him, she rode oblivious to the dangerous trail.

It wasn't until Oscar pulled his horse to a halt, dismounted, and stopped the train that Ashley shook away the reverie. She realized a cut in the cliff had allowed the trail to broaden slightly.

"We'll rest the animals here," Oscar shouted to the others back along the line.

Ashley slid to the ground and nearly fell. Her feet and legs were numb. To keep her balance, she clung to the horse's mane while the feeling returned to her limbs. She patted and smoothed the animal's neck while examining the mountainside. Lining the vee that had been cut naturally by spring run-offs, all she could see was brushy growth whose color had turned and faded in the late autumn. Her father and the others were out of sight. She could see no farther back than Davey's burro.

"That's aspen," Quinn said as he and Davey walked back to join her. "We've had an unusually late fall, or the leaves would already be off." He pointed to the mountain. "Use those rocks for ladder steps and this cut takes you clear to the top of the mountain." He paused. "It's a hike we'll have to take. The view from on top is awe inspiring." He spoke distinctly and loudly enough for Oscar to hear every word.

She smiled at him, taking care this time to keep any emotion from showing in her eyes. It was difficult, for she knew she would very much like to take that hike with Mr. Jones. She regarded him from under lowered lids. Perhaps if she thought of him only as a nameless miner, she could keep her emotions disciplined. "I'd like that," she said, adopting an aloof manner. In spite of her resolve, though, her gaze slid to his and locked. Her heart lifted. "I'd like it very much."

He flashed her a boyish grin. Then, slowly he dropped his eyes and looked down at Davey. "Come on, son, let's go check our mounts." His voice had lost its firmness. The words came out tremulous and hoarse.

Ashley's heart filled her eyes, and she quickly shielded their message from Quinn. She lectured herself with stern reminders to keep her heart and head under control. *Ashley Ferguson, remember why this man's even talking to you and be grateful he's saving you from the lust of these terrible outlaws. Don't make his life more difficult than you already have.*

At length, Oscar bawled, "All right, mount up!" He swung into his saddle and trained his gun on the prisoners as they obeyed his orders.

Quinn boosted Davey onto his mule. Then, without looking at her, Quinn led Ashley's horse to a large boulder where he helped her to mount.

"This narrow trail is about four miles long," Quinn said. "Then it widens some, and it's another two miles to Harmer City."

His voice, controlled and unemotional, left her feeling confused again. He seemed practiced at turning his emotions on and off like a spigot.

"We're nearly a third of the way," Quinn continued. "We'll all be fine if Oscar continues this pace."

Though the words seemed aimed more at Oscar than her, she nodded and said firmly, "I have marveled at the courage and skill necessary to construct a trail into this country, especially one this narrow."

Quinn smiled sardonically. "It's amazing what can be accomplished when gold is at stake. There's even talk of bringing a narrow gauge railroad into the San Juans. The men seem to have the capital to back their dreams. One thing for certain—the first man to drive a railroad into this high country will have his fortune assured, no matter what it costs him to get the track up here." He let his eyes scan the steep walls of the gorge. "I don't think it will ever happen, though."

Oscar gave Quinn a look of disgust. "Railroads have been built into places worse than this. Men determined to get gold do incredible things."

"That's true," Quinn replied as he swung up onto his horse. "I've seen mine shafts drifted into the face of cliffs so steep the crews needed steel ladders and steam hoists to reach the tunnels. Working a shaft like that would be difficult enough, but can you imagine what it took to *find* the vein in the first place? Boggles the mind when you consider it."

They rode on, Quinn pointing out things of interest to Ashley. Under different circumstances, she would have enjoyed his running commentary. Now, however, she kept wondering how her father was faring. Also, she had heard or seen nothing of Sidell or Litch since entering the trail. Were they still behind her, or had they found another shortcut the way they did with the stage? Had they ridden ahead to lie in wait? Could she expect a well-placed bullet to pierce her at any moment?

She glanced over the edge of the trail and quickly shrank back. She didn't want to consider what would happen if a horse or mule balked or took a false step.

Quinn was giving a flawless performance of the loving and concerned husband and father. Setting aside her worries, she tried to enjoy their growing comradarie. It took constant prompting to remember their relationship was temporary.

"We're about a mile from the end," Quinn called to Oscar. "Last cut up ahead has a spring running into a small pool before it seeps away into the rocks. Good place to water the animals."

Just as Oscar acknowledged Quinn's information with a brief nod, Ashley saw a flicker of movement followed for a second by a grey, flowing shape. A rabbit? She didn't have time to ask. Whatever it was, Quinn's horse flattened his ears against his head and with a squeal of terror, the big gelding reared.

Ashley gasped. There was no room for the animal to act up. She watched, helpless, as the chestnut, balancing on its hind legs, pawed the air and inched backward toward the edge of the trail.

"Father—please—save Mr. Jones!" she whispered as her heart tightened and leaped into her throat. Clenching her own reins in a death grip, Ashley willed Quinn's horse to return all four feet to the trail.

The bitter taste of fear filled her mouth, and Ashley swallowed hard against the scream choking her. She fought the inclination to clench her knees into her own horse. Her tight hold on the reins forced the gelding's head down and inward toward the wall.

Kicking free of his stirrups, Quinn boosted himself over the cantle of the saddle. He slid free down the horse's rump. As he fell clear of the terrified animal, though, Quinn reeled out of balance, his arms flailing in a vain search for a handhold on the slick, rock wall. Quinn stumbled and sprawled backward onto the narrow lip of trail. Fighting for balance his head and shoulders extended out into space.

Only feet away, Quinn's horse came down to all fours. Its back foot skidded over the edge, and the animal panicked. Mindless with terror, the gelding tried to spin around and race down the trail. But there was no room on the narrow shelf for such a large animal to turn. In the attempt to fling itself away from the sheer drop, the horse rammed a hoof into Quinn. Quinn spun out of control again. Teetering on the edge of the trail, he fought desperately to regain his balance.

The crazed horse, thrashing to turn around, lunged wildly and slammed into Quinn again. It planted its feet in air far out over the edge of the dropoff. Then, without a sound, the animal disappeared.

Quinn, staggered by the blow, tried to throw himself to the inside of the trail, away from the rim of the abyss. But he was too far off-balance. For an instant he pirouetted on the heel of one boot like a ballerina on point. His fingers clutched the air as he grabbed for a handhold.

There was nothing to hold on to.

His long body extended out over the cliff as though reaching after the fallen horse, Quinn, too, disappeared.

Below lay nothing but deadly rocks and foaming, wild water a hundred feet down. The reverberating roar of the raging torrent as it churned and roiled over the great ragged rocks filled the canyon.

The scream escaped Ashley's tortured throat as a low moan.

Chapter 7

Slowly, Quinn came around. His head throbbed. His body ached. With each intake of air, such stabbing pains shot through his back that he breathed as seldom and as shallowly as possible. He thought he must have been unconscious for some time, but he couldn't be sure. He wasn't sure about anything except that he hurt all over. Did that mean he wasn't dead? But he must be. Anyone falling the distance he had and landing on those boulders in the bottom of the canyon would surely be dead.

He stirred slightly. Though his head and ribs ached the worst, pain streaked through him everywhere. He opened his eyes and found his vision foggy. Things were dark and shadowlike. *Oh, dear Lord,* he prayed. *Don't let me be blind, please.* He tried to determine if the blurred darkness was a result of injury or the time of day. *Probably a combination of both,* he decided.

Trying to clear his vision, he shook his head. That was a mistake. Through the roar in his ears, he heard a moan.

Waves of fresh pain washed through him.

Still, the attack of intense pain brought him to full consciousness. He tried to sit up and almost fell again.

Almost fell again! His heart thudded with the realization. How could he almost fall if he lay at the bottom of the canyon? With a surge of desperate strength, he grabbed a large rock next to him.

Fully aware now, Quinn clung with all his might to the handhold. He let his eyes explore the situation.

By some miracle, he had fallen onto a narrow shelf of rock protruding from the sheer cliff face. Quinn sprawled precariously above the canyon floor. *The Lord surely protected me*, Quinn thought.

Looking down the sheer wall beneath that eyebrow of a trail, Quinn realized the drop to the bottom was unobstructed except for the narrow, protruding ledge that held him. Far below he could see his horse lying still and broken on the rocks near the swiftly running river.

Peering up, he could see nothing but the flat, glistening surface of the rock wall and the blue sky. He must have fallen more than thirty feet. Below him, it had to be at least another hundred feet to the boulder-strewn stream bed.

Peering over the edge of the knob again, he carefully studied the scene. He swallowed hard, giving thanks once more for the grace of the Lord that had saved him.

Strangely, Quinn couldn't hear the churning rumble of the racing water. Once more he shook his head to dislodge the roar filling his ears. Pain sliced knife-like through his brain. Another moan escaped him.

Quinn tried to swallow, but his throat seemed glued together. He stared with great longing at the cold water rushing in such quantities below him. He tried to imagine some of it passing over his lips and down his parched throat.

Are you going to lie here and die without a fight? he goaded himself. *Water's not going to flow up to you.*

Ignoring the pain it induced, he inched himself to a sitting position and started looking for a way down. That was when the full force of his situation hit him. He had nothing to help him get down . . . or up.

Where was the pack train? What must Davey think? Davey! Quinn choked on a sob as he thought of the silent little boy believing he was an orphan once again.

And Ashley. Without him to defend her, she would be at the mercy of Sidell and Litch. Anger rose in him, and the rapid breathing it caused sent sickening jabs of pain through his midsection. *Lord, please protect her. Don't blame her for my sin. I know I shouldn't have sprung so quickly to a lie earlier. You always have an honest way to work. I just couldn't think of another way to protect her. Forgive me for my hasty words, and please keep her safe,* he prayed. Her face rose before him, and he knew it would be very easy to love the elegant Lady Ashley.

He commanded his mind to return to his predicament. Surely someone would come for him. But who? He reviewed the possibilities. Under the guns of the outlaws, Jake, Will and Riley were helpless. Sidell and Litch were totally without feeling. Quinn knew he could expect no sympathy from that source.

Though Oscar was a cruel and dangerous man, at times he seemed more human than the rest. Quinn gave a dry laugh and winced with the pain. *You're kidding yourself, Quinn. With you out of the way, their chances of getting to that vug have increased mightily.*

But Jake would try to persuade them to organize a search. Surely Jake wouldn't let him die without attempting a rescue.

Then it occurred to Quinn that no one knew he was alive. He tried to call, but over the roaring in his ears, he couldn't tell if any sound issued from his tortured throat. Nothing seemed to penetrate the throbbing rumble in his head.

If everyone thought him dead, they had probably gone

on. It could have been hours since he fell. He could very well be here alone and forgotten. Briefly, he rested his feverish brow against the cool rock and prayed for courage and strength. Without the Lord, he was not going to get out of this alive. The cold realization that they thought him dead settled in his mind. Even if his body wasn't visible from the trail, they would suppose he had fallen out of sight into a crevice. Had Quinn watched the plunge he took, he would not have believed anyone could have survived. How could he expect the others to think he had?

Quinn began an assessment of his injuries. He found a few shallow cuts and scratches which had already stopped bleeding. Gingerly he flexed his arms and legs. There seemed to be no broken bones there. His ribs, however, were another matter. The pain that even shallow breathing caused told him something was drastically amiss in his midsection.

His head pounded with pulsing regularity, the pain centering in the back of his head. Cautiously he examined the focus of the pain and found a large knot. *Probably cracked my skull. Goes to show my head isn't as hard as I thought it was.*

No matter. He had to move if he was going to get out of this mess. Fighting against the grey haze that swam across his eyes, Quinn inched himself to his knees. He tried to feel the surface of the cliff and realized he still wore his riding gloves. Pressing his trembling, pain-wracked body against the damp face of the cliff, Quinn, with fingers made clumsy by cold, removed his gloves. He ran the tips of his fingers over the rock above him, searching for knobs and cracks to use as hand and toe holds. He did not relish this climb. Not the way he felt— weak and sick and dizzy, hurting all over.

But, since everyone thought him dead, climbing was the only way off this knob. It had to be attempted. With dogged determination, he searched for anything to help him cling to the rock.

His desperate fingers encountered nothing but slick, smooth granite. He could neither see nor feel anything that promised hope. He moaned his despair. For the first time, Quinn accepted that he was trapped here.

Drawing a shallow, trembling breath, he closed his eyes and pressed his face against the gritty cliff face. This wasn't the way he wanted his life to end.

And what about Davey? Who would look after him? Give him the love and understanding he needed? Jake was good to the boy, a fine grandfather, but not a father.

Once again Quinn allowed his thoughts to turn to Ashley. Maybe she had been blown into his path in Durango for a reason. She seemed to understand Davey, and the boy responded well to her. Quinn had a feeling Ashley would be a warm, caring mother, if she chose to stay. That comforted him. He refused to think that she would take Davey and leave the mountains.

Ashley was uncommonly brave and uncomplaining. Obviously used to luxuries he probably hadn't heard of, she had not uttered a single, grumbling word about the inconveniences and crudities life in this country imposed on its inhabitants and guests. Even now he could scarcely believe she had foregone the warmth and comfort inside the stagecoach to ride on top in the storm.

He thought of her sitting next to him, and let the remembrance drift through his mind. He pictured her kind, smiling face. It pleased him. He saw her long, dark eyelashes. They rested demurely against pale, flawless skin drawn tightly to reveal high cheekbones, then without warning they swept up to reveal large, blue-violet eyes. He especially liked her eyes. Sometimes they sparked with indignation, then as quickly changed and glowed with tenderness. Turning wide and innocent, they sent messages of trust. The effect undid him emotionally.

Hope stirred. Ashley wouldn't let them leave him behind. But then, as quickly as it had arisen, that bit of wishful thinking flickered and died. What did he think she could do? She might be wonderful, but she was no match against gold hungry bandits.

His knees began to ache. Even the thought of moving made beads of perspiration rise on his forehead, but he couldn't stay crouched as he was. *The Lord didn't provide this ledge just to let you die, Quinn Jones. If He'd wanted to do that, He could have let you fall all the way.* So, bracing himself, Quinn eased into a sitting position. Wrapping his arms around his pain-shot middle, he rested his aching head against the cool rocks.

He had no idea how long he sat like that, resting against the pain, when a scraping sound on the rocks above roused him. He listened intently, but all he could hear was the roar in his ears. *Probably imagined you heard something, old boy. Gotta watch that wishful thinking.*

Quinn shivered as the cool breeze started up. It was late afternoon. Quinn grimaced. It was going to be a long night. He rested his head against the cold rock and made his mind a blank.

He jerked up with a start. *Had* he heard something? He listened intently, but the only sound he could be sure of was the creek thrashing below.

There it was again! He hadn't imagined the noise. It sounded like horseshoes scraping against rocks on the trail above.

The deep rumble filling his head seemed less. Maybe he was hearing again. He sat forward, held his breath, and listened intently. Though he listened for a long time, all he heard was the roar inside his ears.

He crumpled back against the rock, disappointment squeezing out the brief hope. Obviously, he had imagined the sounds.

But what if he hadn't? He sat up straight again and breathed deeply despite the pain. "Hello!" he called. "You up there! *Hello!*" The words rasped and caught in his dry throat. Quinn tried to yell again, but only succeeded in

98

making a thin, ragged croak.

Rocks rattled overhead! Hooves pounded on the trail above him! Once more Quinn tried to yell. He coughed from the strain, then tried again. "Hello up there!" Better, but obviously still not loud enough to be heard since the hoofbeats continued steadily along the path.

Maybe they couldn't remember the exact spot he went over. It would soon be dark. Would they give up the search? Torturing himself with these thoughts, Quinn moaned.

Quinn, get hold of yourself. Think! Maybe he could toss something up onto the trail that would attract their attention. He looked about, but there was nothing he could lift, much less throw that far.

Was it his imagination, or had the hoofbeats slowed and turned back?

Straining, he could hear nothing more. Either the horses had stopped directly above him . . . or they had never existed at all. Craning his neck, he tried to peer up. From where he lay, it was impossible to see any part of the narrow trail above. It could easily be empty.

Only silence echoed overhead. He could hear nothing beyond the lessening roar inside his head.

He tried again when he could bear the pain and catch enough breath. "Hello!" At least, he was able to hear that faint croaking sound so his hearing wasn't completely gone.

"Did you hear something?" Ashley's voice carried to his precarious position.

Relief washed over Quinn. He had known she wouldn't leave him!

"Probably just the wind," Jake answered.

Quinn stretched upward and moaned with the agony the act produced. "No! It's not the wind. It's me!" he croaked in broken syllables.

"What are you two mumbling about?" came Oscar's cold voice.

"We aren't mumbling," Ashley retorted. "I think I heard something down below."

"Well, I didn't. Besides, dead men don't talk."

"Mr. Jones is not dead," Ashley said. "I know he's alive, and he's right beneath us."

"You're right, Ashley. I'm caught down here and I can't move. Throw me a rope!" Quinn didn't have the strength to yell, but if sound traveled up as clearly as it traveled down, they should be able to hear him.

"There! Did you hear that? I know he's down there and alive." Her voice was filled with urgency. "Hurry! He's probably terribly injured. It's beginning to grow cold, Mr. Oscar. We must reach him at once if he is to be saved."

There was a pause and a series of rustling, clinking sounds. Moments later Quinn could see Jake's head and shoulders.

"Here!" Quinn called in a hoarse rasp. "Over here, Jake!"

"Well, I'll be a . . . ! You hang on there, boy. We'll think of some way to get you up." His head and shoulders disappeared. "Quinn's right below us. Caught on a knob of rock. Don't look real good, but he's alive."

Two heads appeared. Quinn ignored Oscar's ugly face and concentrated on Ashley. Her worried countenance gladdened his heart. She did care about him.

"Oh, Mr. Jones, how are you?" she called.

"Much better now that you're here," he told her. "How's Davey?"

"Unresponsive. If it registered what happened, he's making no show of it," she answered.

Jake's head pushed into Quinn's sight. "We'll get you up somehow. Hold on a little longer."

"Don't think I'm going anywhere." Quinn's tight, dry throat broke his words into weak croaks. His voice sounded foreign to his ears.

The heads disappeared. Quinn waited and listened to scrapes, jangles, and sounds he couldn't identify.

100

Occasionally Ashley or Jake would lean over the edge and buoy up Quinn's spirits with words of encouragement. Beyond that, the time passed with no tangible signs of rescue. Quinn grew more cold and stiff in the descending chill of evening, and their words of reassurance sounded increasingly hollow. He began to believe that they were hiding the truth from him. They couldn't reach him. Then, he heard the distinctive sounds of hammer on metal.

"Keep a sharp eye out, Quinn, my boy," Jake hollered down. "Here comes the rope."

Quinn looked up to see a coil of new rope snake its way down over the edge of the trail. He groaned when the rope fell at least five feet from him. There was no way he could reach it.

The rays of the setting sun caught Jake's silver hair as he leaned dangerously far out over the cliff and called down to Quinn. "We had to anchor the pins where we could find a crevice to work from. I'll get the rope over to you. Think you can tie yourself to it?"

"I could try climbing it . . . . "

"Don't you even think of such a thing!" Ashley's voice cut him off as she joined Jake in leaning out into space.

At the sight of the danger she was in, Quinn's heart stuttered in its beating. "Ashley, get back on that trail before you fall," he ordered in a voice whose strength surprised him. "There isn't room on this ledge for company."

Ashley smiled a twisted little smile and pulled back out of sight.

Quinn breathed a sigh of relief.

"She's right, son," Jake called. "Don't try climbing. You might not be able to do it. Then we'd lose you for sure. There's a loop in the end. Tie yourself in and we'll pull you up."

Quinn stared at the dangling loop. There was no way Jake and Ashley could hoist his body up that ledge. He knew Oscar wouldn't help. "The two of you can't lift me," he protested.

The rope danced closer to him. Quinn reached out and snagged it. Jake leaned out, watching, while Quinn pulled the loop over his head. He secured it around his chest, each movement a pain-filled second of time. "Got it," he called at last, breathless and only semi-conscious from the rush of agony through his head and chest.

Jake's head disappeared. Quinn felt the rope tighten until it dug painfully into his back. At least the pressure was above the ribs he guessed were broken. He gave silent thanks.

"Pull now," Ashley instructed Jake.

Quinn felt the rope gouge deeper, squeezing the breath from his body as it raised him up and away from the heaven-sent shelf which had caught him. For a few feet he scrubbed along the side of the abrasive granite wall. Then, the lift was straight up until he finally reached the edge of the trail.

As Quinn's head cleared the edge of the trail, he could see the hoist they had rigged. Into the cliff wall, Jake had driven a series of metal pegs with steel rings attached and then connected them to a pulley.

Thank you, Lord, for Jake's years of mining experience, Quinn thought as he swung onto the trail and tried to stand. He caught only a glimpse of Oscar leaning against the slick rock wall with a pistol leveled at Ashley before the pain shooting through him turned his knees to jelly, and he crumpled. The faint fragrance of an expensive perfume told him that the body he had collapsed against and the strong arms lowering him to the ground were Ashley's.

Chapter 8

Slowly Quinn opened his eyes and looked up into a stand of gold-tinted aspen towering overhead, making a protective canopy as their tops intertwined. He was stretched out on a bed of pine boughs and covered with several blankets. Nearby, Jake tended a small fire. Oscar kept his vigil while slumped in a relaxed position atop a gnarled and weathered fallen log. Ashley, her back to Quinn, fussed over a satchel.

Quinn tried to sit up and gasped. Something sharp pierced his chest. He flinched with the pain and, though he clenched his teeth in an attempt to stifle any sound, a soft moan escaped.

Ashley whirled. "You lie down and stay there," she ordered. "Those ribs need to be bound. Keep moving about and you'll send one into a lung. Then, only surgery will help, and I'm not that skilled."

With a sheepish grin, he obeyed. It was incredible how much better he felt, knowing she was taking care of him.

His nose wrinkled. "Is that coffee I smell?"

"Thought you might like some," Jake said, removing tin cups from a pack box. "Or would you rather have plain water?"

"Jake, right now I'd drink anything."

"Coffee's not quite ready. Guess you'll have to do with lukewarm water." Jake twisted the cap off a canteen and brought it to Quinn.

Quinn took several deep swallows, rested, then drained the container.

Jake looked carefully at Quinn. "You look better."

"I feel a whole lot better."

Ashley appeared with a handful of wide cloth strips and knelt beside him. "This is going to make you feel even better."

"Thanks for coming back," Quinn said.

Her eyes widened, their color deepening to twilight blue. "Did you actually think we would leave you? What kind of barbarians do you take us for?"

Quinn's eyes shifted to Oscar who watched the scene with passive disinterest.

"Well, we did have a bit of a time persuading Mr. Oscar that you must be rescued," she confessed and cast a jaundiced eye at Oscar. "Mr. Jones, are you up to sitting? I'm going to have to take off your coat and shirt."

He wasn't up to moving, much less sitting, but he would be hanged before Ashley found out. He tensed against the anticipated stabs of pain.

"Here, let me help you," Ashley said and slipped an arm under his shoulders. "Mr. Harmer, would you please assist Mr. Jones on the other side?"

With the two of them doing the work of his bruised muscles, Quinn managed to sit up without blacking out. A slick film of perspiration sheathed his body, and the cold of evening intensified the effect. He shivered and the act sent more fingers of pain through him.

"Sit as straight as possible," Ashley instructed as she

began wrapping the white strips of sheeting around his midsection.

She wants me to sit straight, Quinn thought as his vision blurred and Ashley's voice faded in and out. *She'll be lucky if I don't pass out cold.*

"Here, boy, lean against me," Jake said.

Quinn felt the old man's hand on his shoulder. It guided him back against Jake's body. Keeping his midsection straight, gratefully Quinn leaned his weight against Jake. "Thanks," Quinn whispered.

In the manner of any good doctor, Ashley began visiting with her patient. "You seem to have quite a reputation for accurate shooting and successful fighting. Oscar let us know he was most relieved that you had been removed as a threat. Jake convinced him, however, that you were indispensable in locating the golden room."

Jake reached out and shoved another log on the fire. "Told him I didn't even know where that gold strike was. Reasons of security and all."

Quinn cast a glance at Oscar to see how he was taking Jake's comments. The deceptively pleasant looking man sat with his body rigid and his face blank. His eyes glittered a dangerous black, however, and he shot a deadly look at Jake.

"I counted on Oscar's greed as well as the possibility that there might still be a little humanity alive in the old boy," Jake continued, ignoring Oscar's looks. "Turned out I was right. Oscar finally sent the others along to Harmer City, and we came back here with a supply burro. Lucky for us when Will was in town delivering the ore to the mill, he picked up the very things we needed to rescue you."

Quinn glanced up at Jake. "Wasn't luck. Only the Lord kept me from joining my horse on the rocks." Turning to Oscar, Quinn stared hard at him. "I am, however, also beholden to you for allowing them to come back for me."

Oscar rose from his log and walked slowly to where

Quinn lay on the ground. "Indeed you are, and I don't plan on letting you forget it. Besides, I couldn't take the chance the old man was telling the truth about you bein' the only one to know where the gold room is. I don't consider you much of a threat in that condition."

"You're right about that," Quinn agreed as Oscar started to walk away.

Ashley gave a hard tug on the wrapping to tighten it.

Struggling to keep his face from twisting in pain, Quinn smothered a moan.

"Mr. Jones! I'm so sorry," Ashley said. "It is not my intent to hurt you." She paused and bit her lower lip while she wiped away the beads of perspiration which had appeared suddenly on his forehead. "But I know no other way to wrap you." Her sympathy deepened the blue of her eyes and Quinn determined to keep his pain to himself if it choked him.

Jake leaned over and studied Quinn's face. "Boy must be hurt real bad," he whispered, as though Quinn couldn't hear.

Before Ashley could answer, Oscar walked over to glare down at Quinn. "All right, that's enough chitty-chat. Haven't you about got him ready to travel yet? Sun's down and we still got some miles to the camp."

Ashley frowned over her shoulder at the scowling man. "As soon as I get his shirt back on, Mr. Jones will be as ready as I can make him under the circumstances."

Jake leaned forward and said softly, "You goin' to be able to get up, boy, or are we going to have to carry you to the horse?"

"You stand up real slow, Mr. Harmer," Oscar ordered in a hard voice. "Then step away from Jones and the lady. Don't need you three hatching up something." Oscar drew a second pistol from its holster and held it on Jake. Turning back to Ashley, he said, "Get Jones up onto that dun gelding and be quick about it."

Quinn pressed his lips into a grim line and waved

Ashley away. *I'll get to my feet alone if it kills me.*

He struggled to stand up while daggers of pain knifed through his midsection. Though he fought valiantly, the pain sickened him. He slumped down onto his hands and knees.

"You planning to crawl to the camp?" Oscar asked, his voice harsh with contempt. "Seems a hard way to get there, but make your choice. We're leaving now, with or without you." His gun discharged, sending a ball of light out the barrel. The bullet whipped through Ashley's wind-billowed skirt and cut the back of Quinn's right boot top. Its force pulled him off balance and with a sharp cry, he crumpled into the dirt face first.

Jake let out a roar and took a step in Quinn's direction.

"You stand where you are, old man!" Oscar snapped. He reinforced his words with a wave of his gun in Jake's direction.

Ashley spun until she faced Oscar. Her face white, she clenched her hands against her anger. "Have you gone completely mad?" she cried. Dropping beside Quinn, with trembling fingers, Ashley examined the bullet hole. "The bullet went straight through your boot," she said. "Didn't even graze your leg." She bit her trembling lower lip, unable to speak as anger faded, and she absorbed the shock of Oscar's act.

Unaided, Quinn struggled back onto his hands and knees. He tried to give her a reassuring smile, but it turned into a cynical twist of his upper lip. "It's all right," he whispered brokenly. Like a giant bear, he swayed on unsteady limbs. Rising nausea and pain threatened to draw him into unconsciousness. He clamped his teeth against the fresh waves of agony. He pleaded silently with his heavenly Father for control. "Take my arm," he ordered Ashley.

Giving Oscar a venomous look, silently Ashley helped Quinn lever himself onto his feet. Though he tried not to, he found himself leaning heavily on her.

They made their way with tortured slowness the short distance across the uneven ground toward the horses. Each step required a supreme effort. By the time they halted in front of the horse, Quinn's shirt was drenched in perspiration, and beads gathered on his forehead and ran into his eyes.

Ashley reached into her jacket pocket and took out a small linen handkerchief. She dabbed his dripping face.

"All right, all right," Quinn protested softly. "Help me up, Ashley." He reached out and stroked the gelding's nose. "Now, fella, hold still while I mount."

His speech was oddly slurred, both surprising and frightening him. "How about letting Jake give me a hand?" Quinn asked Oscar.

"You two are doing just fine. I'll keep the old duffer here as insurance against either of you trying something fancy."

Although anger blazed through Quinn, he looked down at Ashley and managed a wan smile. "You'd better land me on that horse the first time, ma'am. Turn the stirrup so I can get my left foot in it, then get under me and boost."

Quinn waited while Ashley turned the stirrup toward him. Grasping the saddle horn with his right hand, Quinn lifted his left leg. Ashley guided the stirrup toward his boot. Then swiftly, as Quinn pulled on the horn, she pushed from behind. Quinn levered himself over the cantle and into the saddle.

Sitting on the horse was a sustained agony, and the look in Ashley's eyes said she knew it. She spoke nothing, however. Handing him the reins, she moved his boot out of the stirrup. Then she pulled herself up behind Quinn.

Once Ashley was settled behind him, Quinn signaled the horse into a walk. Slowly they traveled the narrow trail up the windy slit between the mountains. Great granite peaks, mauled by the weather until the sparse trees splintered, towered in evening-darkened splendor. Burned trunks bore mute evidence of the lightning slashed storms that rolled through the country. Giant boulders, split off the high peaks, lined the trail. Others had rolled down the steep walls and buried themselves deep in the stream bottom. Quinn shuddered at the thought of that stream bottom and how close he had come to death.

Their pace was slow and, finally, he could fight the pain no longer. His head lolled forward onto his chest, and he felt himself slip sideways in the saddle. He felt Ashley put her arms around his waist to keep him in the saddle. At last she slipped the reins from his hands and guided the horse.

Ashley. He owed her his life. He should keep his distance. If he didn't watch out, he'd be falling in love with her.

Frustration welled inside him. Life was indeed strange, promising so much, withholding more. Though he had wealth beyond his grandest dreams, the love of Lady Ashley Ferguson could never be his. He knew he could never leave these mountains and be happy, and she couldn't survive their rigors. Quinn knew that in time she would come to hate him for having made her a prisoner in a foreign world. He had seen it happen over and over again. His features twisted into a grimace. No, any thought of Ashley beyond that necessary to see her safely on her way must be thoroughly strangled.

Besides, he had no idea of where she stood with the Lord.

With a small sigh, he leaned back against her. Feeling her strength, he drew comfort, thanked the Lord for that, and slipped into semi-consciousness.

Chapter 9

Harmer City, named for its founder, came as a shock to Ashley. Expecting a few rough board hovels clinging to a nearly vertical mountainside, she was astounded as they rode within sight of a real town. Well, not London, of course, but still, compared to the deserted mining villages she had seen in California and Nevada, Harmer City was a thriving little community. In the last light still streaking the night sky, she could see one street of log structures and on the hill above them, a large log house.

Arriving at a trail which turned up the hill off the main road, Jake dropped back to ride next to Quinn and Ashley. Worry furrowed Jake's brow. "How's Quinn doing?" he asked.

"I think he's been unconscious most of the time. He's riding by instinct. How much farther to the house?"

"It's up there." Jake pointed.

"That fine house on the side of the mountain?"

Jake nodded and a shy smile broke through.

Ashley was impressed. "Except that it is made of logs, it looks like as fine a mansion as any I've seen here in America," Ashley said softly.

He chuckled. "Be sure to repeat those remarks when Quinn's awake. Such praise will make him a happy man. He helped a great deal in the building of my house."

A tattoo of hooves slid to a halt next to Ashley. "What are you two talking about?" Oscar ground the words between his teeth and waved his gun at her.

Ashley refused to let him see how he frightened her. *Please, Father, give me the strength to see this night through.* Holding her shoulders in a forward rigid posture, she turned only her head and glared at Oscar. "I was merely commenting on Mr. Harmer's fine house," she said in a firm voice.

"I don't need any smart talk from a society snob like you," Oscar retorted. "Now, ride!" To accent his order he reached over and jabbed the gun in Quinn's ribs.

Quinn gave a sharp cry and slipped sideways in the saddle despite Ashley's efforts to hold him. Jake reached out to lend a steadying hand.

"Oscar, you're a sharp man with a gun, but you know Quinn's reputation," Jake said, his anger barely controlled. "If you value your life, you'll not anger him any more'n you already have."

At Jake's words, Ashley felt Quinn stiffen and his head jerked up.

"Oh, my, my, my . . . I am upset," Oscar said mockingly. "Now, get up that trail!"

When they arrived at the house, Jake leaped off his burro and hurried to help Ashley. Looking at Oscar, he said, "Ease Quinn off and help him into my study. He can sleep there until he heals enough to climb the stairs to his . . . . their room."

Oscar kept the gun trained on them. "Just who are you giving orders to?"

Jake winced. "Sorry. Forgot myself there for a minute." Anxiously he eyed Quinn, who was white-faced and had slumped forward in the saddle.

Turning her back on Oscar, Ashley slid to the ground and studied Quinn. Though he was trying valiantly to hide it, his ordeal had left him far less than the robust man who had started from Durango. She guessed his knees wouldn't be reliable once he stood.

"By any standards, that was quite a fall Mr. Jones took," she said. "Perhaps if we brought the horse nearer the steps, he could dismount without so much jarring."

Jake started to move the horse.

"Hold it!" Oscar pulled his horse up until he towered over Ashley.

Her heart leaped in fear and pounded in her ears, but she kept a firm grip on Quinn.

Oscar pursed his lips and surveyed the scene. "Jones doesn't look real good, does he?" he said, at last. "Be a shame to lose our number one hostage and never find out where that gold is." He took the reins from Jake and led the gelding to the steps.

Ashley held out hands to steady him, but Quinn shook off her offer. He managed to slide onto the veranda, but swayed like a toppling oak when he took his first step. "I'm caving in," Quinn whispered in a thin voice. Jake grabbed him, and Ashley rushed up the steps to help.

Quinn leaned heavily on them both as they supported him across the veranda and into the house.

Once inside the foyer, Ashley found the house even more impressive. The place was huge. The log walls in the foyer had been planed smooth and the cream-colored wood gleamed under coats of varnish. Lighted lamps, both hanging and wall-mounted, cast a warm glow over the spotless interior.

"Great sorrow of my life is not having any chandeliers," Jake said, shaking his head sadly. "Can't get 'em up here on the back of a pack mule."

"Frankly, Mr. Harmer, I think they would be out of place," Ashley assured him as her gaze swept the room. "The lamps are of the finest quality and are a perfect accent for the native wood furnishings."

Jake fairly beamed.

Ashley's eyes rested on the sofas, massive and masculine, created out of necessity here in Harmer City, and fitted with dark wine-red velvet pillows rather than permanent upholstery. She and Jake moved Quinn toward one of the comfortable looking sofas.

However, Oscar's mouth began to twitch, and his eyes narrowed to black pinpoints. He waved the hand holding the gun, a signal for them to move on.

Jake steered Quinn across the room to a thick, carved door. In the silence, their feet echoed on the highly polished hardwood floor.

Quinn's color rapidly changed to a sickly chalk white. A blue line rimmed his compressed lips. He tucked his left arm tightly against his side as though pressure might ease the pain walking created.

Ashley threw open the door. The other four gunmen lounged about the room in deceptive nonchalance, pistols bristling from steady hands. The hostages sat like morose statues until they saw Quinn. Exclamations of happy surprise greeted him.

A lanky, homely woman with greying hair drawn in a knot so tight it raised her eyebrows looked up from serving coffee. "Quinn!" she gasped. Setting the pitcher down with a crash, she rushed to help him. "Ain't really you, is it? Everyone said you fell off the trail and over the cliff."

"It's me, Molly. What's left, anyway," Quinn said softly.

"Well, I'll be . . . !" Sidell exclaimed. "Know'd ya was too

113

ornery ta die that easy. Molly, get over here with that coffee. Jones got enough sympathy with his wife hoverin' over him."

Slumped in a chair, Lord Peter looked slightly dazed, but not physically worse for his experience. At the sight of Ashley, relief spread over his face, and he squared his shoulders. "Thank heaven, Mr. Jones, Daughter. The Lord has spared you both."

"Yes, He has, Father. However, Mr. Jones is the one we must have concern for." Ashley helped ease Quinn into a highbacked chair covered with rich brown leather. He sat back, allowing her to remove his boots and place his feet on the footstool.

"Thank you," he whispered as he gave her a weak smile and closed his eyes.

Davey, seated in a straightbacked wooden chair with his feet inches above the floor, followed each movement Ashley made in settling Quinn. Hiller, a great black splotch, lay protectively at Davey's feet. At the sight of Oscar, though, he rose to his haunches and pulled back his lips into a teeth-filled snarl.

Oscar withdrew a step and scowled at Jake. "Somebody better tone down that dog, or I'll put him out of the way. Permanently," he snapped.

Jake hurried to the distraught animal. "Down, Hiller," he crooned. "It's all right, boy."

Hiller's eyes darted from gunman to gunman, leaving no question that he doubted Jake's reassuring words. Hesitantly, however, Hiller sank to a crouch. Davey rested his dangling feet on Hiller's sleek back. The dog relaxed.

"All right, folks, we've been patient long enough," Oscar announced. "Far too long. Sidell, did you find out where that gold is?"

"I tried, but the only two who seem to know anythin' wasn't here."

114

"Well, they are now," Oscar said in cold, clipped syllables. He marched over to where Jake stood. George appeared beside Ashley and placed a pistol at her temple.

Lord Peter started to his feet, but Litch shoved him down and held a gun on him. Ashley closed her eyes and felt a strange calmness come over her. She had had so many harrowing moments in the last two days, she was drained. *Let them shoot. It would be preferable to the constant threat.*

"No!" Quinn's voice held no strength.

Ashley's eyes flew open. Quinn tried to stand, but his knees folded and he crumpled in battered helplessness into the chair.

Oscar laughed. "Not much left of the tough man, is there? Can't even protect his missus." Turning to Jake, he said, "I suggest you tell us real quick where that gold is, or I can't guarantee what George and Gene will do. Their great joy is target practice, and they haven't had much opportunity in the past couple of days."

Gene moved his gun from Riley and Will and took aim at Quinn. George pressed the cold metal of his gun barrel against Ashley's temple. Though she paled under the threat, she regarded Oscar with a steady eye.

"Won't do any good to threaten me," Jake said quietly. "I don't know anything about the gold."

"That's ridiculous. You're the mine owner. Don't tell me your crew found a room full of gold, and you haven't been told," Oscar said.

"That's precisely what I am telling you. If you found a room of gold so pure all you had to do was scrape it off the walls and sell it, would you go rushing off to tell the mine owner?" Jake paused. "You bet your sweet life you wouldn't. You'd keep it a secret, work at night when everyone else was asleep, fill your pokes, and stash 'em somewhere until you could get a way out of here. That is, if

115

such a room has been found."

Casually, Jake dropped into the chair behind his desk and rested his head against its high back. To accent his lack of concern, he calmly began examining his finger-nails. The silence, broken only by the ticking of the ornate floor clock and the soft crackling of a cheery fire in the large rock fireplace, deepened as Oscar weighed Jake's words.

At last, he turned his gun on Quinn. "What about you? How much do you know?"

Quinn remained as he had collapsed. His torso straight, his head lolled against the winged back of the chair, his eyes closed.

"You! Mrs. Jones!" Oscar's voice lashed out. "Bring him around. I want to know where that gold room is."

"If I don't know about any gold, why would you think he would?" Jake asked, his eyes wide with innocence. "While he's my bodyguard and we are rarely separated, he doesn't know all my business."

"Means you don't know all his, either," Oscar retorted quickly.

"Robbing a mine doesn't hardly seem the thing uppermost on the mind of a man off gettin' hisself a beautiful new bride." Jake smiled warmly at Ashley. "Wouldn't be on my mind at all." He cocked his head and squinted his appraisal of Oscar. "Don't believe it'd be foremost on yours, either."

Sidell swaggered up to Davey and leveled a pistol at him. The look of terror that filled Davey's face said he knew exactly what the threat was.

This was too much. Ashley whirled and started for Sidell. "You insane creature, put that gun away this instant, or . . . "

He shifted the aim of his weapon to Ashley. "Or you'll what, lady?" His eyes took on a queer glitter and his finger played over the trigger.

116

Hiller positioned himself into a springing stance, and the tension in the room crackled.

Oscar swore. "Sidell! Get back where you belong."

Sidell's glittering eyes flicked over the room.

Fear and anger radiated from the eyes of the prisoners. Its heated waves pulsed against him.

"Ya think I'd really shoot a kid?" He looked slightly sheepish as he edged away from the scene he had created.

Oscar glared at Sidell. "You sure you know what you're after here? Personally, I'm beginning to doubt there is a gold room."

Sidell turned mean little eyes on Oscar. "Don't recall asking ya to come to this party in the first place. You and yer partners busted in. Ya don't like what yer findin', yer real welcome to ride on out right now."

A slow smile drifted across Oscar's lips. "I know you'd like that, but it's late and I think we'll stay the night, at least." He holstered his gun and turned back to Jake. "How about some food? It's been awhile since my men have eaten."

"It's been awhile since any of us have eaten," Jake said, returning a steady look to Oscar. "Little tough to oblige you with a meal, though. My cook's sitting here under guard."

Oscar paced up and down the room. "You got rooms enough to sleep all of us?" he asked Jake finally.

"Yes, if people double up. Of course, Will has his own cabin and so does Molly."

"They stay here. You going to tell them where to sleep or am I?"

Jake shrugged. "There's a small room off the kitchen. Molly, you can sleep there. Go ahead now, and start fixing something to eat." He looked sideways at Oscar. "I presume that's all right."

"Somebody better get some vittles 'fore we faint from

117

hunger," Sidell snapped.

Oscar looked at Sidell's oversized belly. "You'll survive." He turned to the passengers. "I want you all to understand this. We have had very little sleep the last few nights, and it's catching up with us. Tonight, except for one guard, we will all sleep. Very soundly. If anyone is given to sleepwalking, now is the time to tell me. We'll do you a favor and tie you in bed so you don't get shot." He paused and looked each one in the eye. "Good. Anyone found even trying to get out of his room will be shot, no questions asked. Is that clear?"

"I suppose it's useless to suggest that our things be brought in?" Ashley said with more courage than she felt.

Oscar turned a bland look on her. "That's not an unreasonable request at all. Will and Riley, under Sidell's guard, will start delivering the baggage to your rooms right now. That is, if Jake will ever finish making room assignments." Oscar turned to Molly. "Get going. The kitchen is your domain. Litch, she'll be your responsibility, night and day."

Litch stepped up next to Molly. A nasty gleam sparked in his eyes. Molly gave Litch a cool look and strolled toward the kitchen.

"Hurry it up!" Sidell growled as he fell in to step beside Litch. "Man could starve while ya mosey along." He underscored his words by jabbing his pistol barrel into Molly's back.

She glared at him over her shoulder. "I got a telegram for you, Sidell. You poke me with that thing once more, and I'll see you sleep real sound tonight. Maybe longer."

"Whatcha gonna do, Molly? Huh? Huh?" Sidell laughed loudly and coarsely, making threatening motions with his gun.

"Sidell!" Oscar's voice cracked like a whip across the

118

still room. "Lay off and get back where you were, Molly," he said, and his voice gentled, "if you are behaving yourself, and Sidell is less than courteous at any time during our stay, let me know. I'll see that he learns some manners."

Sidell stepped away from the cook and said nothing. But the venomous look he shot Oscar told clearly of his hatred.

Litch followed Molly out of the study, but he kept his gun out of her back.

"Sidell," Oscar ordered, "see that Will and Riley unload the gear."

Sidell trained his slitted eyes on Oscar and slowly let his gun follow his eyes. George cocked his pistols, covering Sidell.

"That is not a smart move, Sidell. You put a gun on me once more, and I won't stop George."

Sidell gave Oscar a parting glare, then moved to the door. "Come on, Riley, Will," he growled at the two weathered old men lounging easily against the far wall. "Outside!" He threw open the door into the foyer. "Move!" Sidell snapped.

"Seems like them boys is havin' trouble trustin' each other," Riley commented as he pushed himself upright and stepped into the hallway. "Whatta ye think, Will?"

"I think, if I was them, I'd be real careful what I et," Will said casually. "Molly's dynamite with herbs for flavorin' . . . and other things." A sly smile crinkled his face.

Sidell gave no sign of having heard the offhanded remark. He threw open the door onto the porch. "Get out there, you two."

Oscar watched until the little party was outside, then turned to Jake. "Now, help Jones upstairs."

"Oh, please, don't make him climb those stairs, Mr. Oscar," Ashley pleaded. "If a rib slips, it could puncture his lungs, and he would surely die."

Oscar regarded her with a stone face. "Then I suggest

119

you pray that you've done a decent job of binding him up. George, you see that our Englishman, pastor, and businessman get your undivided attention."

George grinned and fanned his gun to indicate he wanted his charges together. "Be on your way, folks," he ordered.

"Gene, you take care of the lady and the kid. And be sure to remind Jones who's in charge here should he forget."

It took all of Ashley's willpower not to shudder under the scrutiny of Gene's pale eyes. They were nearly colorless and bulged from his head, giving him the look of a fish, a dangerous one.

"All right, Jake, get Jones on his feet. Let's go!" Oscar commanded.

Jake leaned over Quinn and shook him gently. That brought only a low groan. "Come on, boy," Jake urged.

"Wait, Mr. Harmer." Ashley felt in her skirt pocket and produced a small vial. "I have some smelling salts. That may revive him enough to walk up the stairs." She waved the strong fumes under Quinn's nose, and he blinked.

With Ashley's help Quinn stood. Held up by Ashley and Jake, he slowly made his way up the broad staircase. Oscar and Gene walked behind, keeping their guns ready.

Jake paused at the first door at the top of the stairs. "This is Mr. and Mrs. Jones' room. Under the circumstances, I would suggest Davey stay with them."

"I agree," Oscar said simply.

Jake helped Quinn onto the bed while Gene followed Ashley and Davey into the large room.

"All right, Harmer, now show the rest of them a bedroom," Oscar ordered.

After Jake and Oscar left, Gene shut the door. In the center of the room was a fragile, rose damask loveseat.

Shuffling over, he plunked down and sprawled his legs in a wide vee.

Ashley drew herself to her nearly six feet. "What do you think you are doing?" Indignation rang through her voice. Acting with feigned boldness, Ashley swept across the room and stepped in front of him. "Outside in the hall, you will be sufficiently close to keep track of our actions. This is the second floor, and in case you haven't noticed, it is a great distance to the ground. I, for one, have no intention of breaking my neck attempting to escape out a window." She marveled at her continued audacity and prayed it wouldn't get them killed. "Guard us if you must, but you will do it from the hallway. We are not having you observe our *every* movement." Storming to the door, she threw it open and pointed a finger. "Out!" she commanded.

If she had slapped him, Gene probably couldn't have looked more startled. His mouth dropped open, but begrudgingly, he gathered his body and stood.

Ashley wondered if she had pushed too hard, but she kept her posture rigid and her stance forbidding. Caving in now would most certainly invite disaster.

"Out!" Ashley ordered again.

Darts of fury shot from under half-shut eyelids as Gene shuffled from the room. He left the door open and sank onto his haunches across the hall from their bedroom.

After giving Davey a reassuring hug and patting Hiller's head, she moved to Quinn's bedside.

She bent over him as he lay sprawled on top of the soft yellow spread. A slick sheen of cold sweat reflected off his pale face. He looked at her with half-shut eyes.

"How do you feel?" she asked.

"I've had better days," he croaked.

She poured a glass of water and held it for him to drink.

"I'll have these clothes off in a moment and get you tucked in. If you can stay awake to eat, I'll bring up a tray as

121

soon as supper is ready."

His eyes widened. "You leave my clothes alone."

Ashley straightened and gave him her coldest eye. "I've been a volunteer for years in the biggest hospital in London. I am quite capable."

"I don't question your capability. You have aptly demonstrated your knowledge." He fixed her with a firm eye. "However, you are *not* taking off my clothes." He spoke with surprising vigor, and seemed ready to continue his defiance of her order when his eyes shifted.

Ashley turned to find Davey, his eyes wide and filled with undisguised confusion, darting from her to Quinn and back again.

"There, see, you've frightened Davey," he accused.

"*I've* frightened Davey? You're the one making the scene."

A scuffing sound at the door drew the attention of both Quinn and Ashley.

"What's goin' on in here?" Gene demanded, waving his gun in Ashley's direction.

Ashley placed her fists on her hips. "If Mr. Jones and I want to discuss his condition, we should certainly have that right without your eavesdropping."

Looking uncomfortable, Gene awkwardly backed away from the room.

Ashley turned to Davey, standing in the middle of the room, his hand buried deep in the hair at the back of Hiller's neck. Great, dark eyes stared from the pale face streaked with dirt and rigid with fear.

Ashley stepped to Davey's side and pulled him next to her. "And now, Davey dear," she continued in a brisk voice. "Let's see how Mr. Jones is doing."

She turned back the bed to find Quinn already under the covers, his pants and shirt in a heap on the floor. As she bent to straighten the quilt, she marveled at the luxury of honest-to-goodness sheets. What she had regarded as

122

a necessity in England was, in this uncivilized land, a prized luxury and not to be taken lightly. Upon further examination, she discovered the mattress and pillows were filled with down feathers. She looked at Quinn, his eyes closed, the pain lines drawing tighter, his slack frame sunk deeply into the soft tick. Her own tired body ached with the longing for such comfort.

However, Davey needed her now. With a weary sigh, she knelt next to him. His eyes, regarding her solemnly, were still confused but highly intelligent. This child was indeed a mystery. Nevertheless, she felt love for him welling inside. She could be a mother to Davey with no effort. "Come, Davey," she said quietly, and took his hand. Hiller stiffened as she touched Davey. "It's all right, Hiller. I want to wash his face and hands. We're going to be eating soon."

As though he understood her words, the great black animal relaxed.

"Here, Davey, sit on the couch. Don't worry about Mr. Jones. He's hurt inside, but we're going to take good care of him, you and I. He's going to be good as new soon."

Davey's eyes were fixed with unwavering intensity on her lips. Seeing this, she spoke slowly and distinctly and soon the little boy's face lit up. "Have you ever panned for gold?" she asked.

A question in his eyes, Davey held his hands as though around a large pan and made swirling motions.

Ashley laughed softly. "Exactly. You do understand what I'm saying."

Davey nodded, and a shy smile settled on his well-shaped lips.

"But you don't speak. Is it because you can't or won't?"

Instantly, the smile faded to be replaced by the thin line Ashley had come to recognize as Davey's retreat. She

123

reached out her arms to him. He drew back and for several minutes eyed her with suspicion. Then he slipped off the sofa and held out his arms in the same way. Smiling widely, Ashley gathered him to her.

Hidden under layers of heavy clothing, the little body was much smaller than she had imagined. Davey snuggled close and Ashley held him until, from the bottom of the stairs, Molly announced supper was served.

The meal was a quiet, tense affair. Over the knot of fear in her throat, Ashley could hardly swallow the ham and biscuits with gravy.

"Mr. Oscar," she finally managed, quaking inside at the audacity of what she was about to request. "Would it be possible for us to, at least, have access to one another's rooms? I need to look after my father, and, of course, Mr. Jones must be cared for during the night."

All the passengers sat rigidly in their chairs watching as Oscar considered her proposal. After what seemed hours, he finally said to Ashley, "I don't suppose it would hurt if you were given the run of the place." He punctuated his words with little jabs of his revolver in her direction. "But bear in mind, Mrs. Jones, you are the *only* one receiving such special treatment. Anyone else will be shot, no questions asked." He sent her a penetrating scowl. "And you will be, too, if you make any one of us nervous."

Oscar looked intently at the other bandits and said, "Hear that, boys? Lady's the *only* one to be moving about."

"Thank you, Mr. Oscar," Ashley said. "Now, if I may be excused, I'd like to prepare a tray for Mr. Jones."

"You finished, Gene?" he asked Ashley's assigned guard.

Gene looked with longing at the cake Molly was carrying in from the kitchen. "Why don't you cut a piece and bring it with you?" Ashley suggested. "I imagine you are fast enough with that gun to thwart any act of mine were I so irresponsible as to attempt something."

Oscar dismissed her with a wave of his hand.

Ashley left the table and hurried into the kitchen where she and Molly readied a tray for Quinn.

Chapter 10

Ashley paused before entering the bedroom. She didn't feel she could go barging into Quinn's room without some warning of her presence. Rebalancing the silver tray, she clattered the utensils.

Licking smears of frosting from his fingers, Gene leaned against the door jamb, carefully eyeing her. "Yer married. Whyn't ya just go in?" Gene asked through a mouthful of cake.

Ashley searched for an excuse. "I . . . I thought Mr. Jones might be asleep, and there's no reason to disturb him if he is."

"If ya thought he was asleep and ya didn't want to wake him, why'd ya bring him food?"

Drat the man. Well, at least Quinn's had enough time not to be caught in an indelicate situation. Dropping her eyelids to conceal her distress, Ashley ignored the question and stepped into the unlit room. Gene's footsteps echoed behind her.

126

Fingers of light from the bracket wall lamps in the hall spread into the murky depths of the bedroom and revealed Quinn sprawled under the covers. His face was a ghostly spectre. With his eyes closed, and arms flung limply out on top of the covers, he looked pitifully weak and defenseless. Her heart sank.

Gene must be arriving at a similar conclusion, Ashley decided as she watched his eyes travel over the helpless figure on the bed. A smirk twitched at Gene's lips.

With trembling hands, she set the tray on the bedside table. "Mr. Jones?" she whispered. Her heart missed a beat when he didn't stir. She looked back at Gene who once more lounged against the door frame licking at his fingers like a cat taking a bath.

The insensitive man infuriated Ashley. She turned her full attention to Quinn. "Mr. Jones, it's me, Ashley. I have some supper for you."

Still, he lay unmoving, only a slight regular lifting of the covers indicating he was even alive.

"Mr. Jones, please say something," she begged.

At last, his eyelids fluttered and in a hoarse croak, he asked, "Who is it?"

"It's Ashley," she said. "Remember?"

A moment of silence, then he said, "Of course, I remember."

She smiled tenderly at him as she fussed with his covers, turning the sheet over the top of the quilt. She eased onto the edge of the bed and lightly stroked back a wayward strand of hair. It lay like a smear of dark chocolate across his forehead. He didn't move at her touch.

"I can see you have little strength, Mr. Jones," she said softly. "However, I have brought you some supper. If you have no objections, I shall feed you."

He made no response to her words.

She asked, "Would you like me to light a lamp?"

"No." With the word shaped by his lips came no sound

127

and even that little effort appeared to cost him more energy than he could spare.

Ashley moved with soft steps to the washstand where she poured water into the basin. Dampening a cloth, she wiped his face and limp hands. She wanted to weep at the weakness in him. When she had doctored him on the trail, she hadn't realized he was so seriously injured. However, she also knew from past experience that a patient often gave up the will to live if the nurse pampered him too much. She had no intention of allowing that to happen with Mr. Jones.

She spread a large linen napkin under Quinn's chin and propped him up with pillows. Then, pulling a chair near the bed, she seated herself. "If you'll open your mouth," she said crisply, "I have some of Molly's delicious chicken noodle soup for you."

"I don't feel like eating," he said in a thin voice so feeble it was barely audible.

Determined to ignore his pitiful rejection, Ashley tested the temperature of the thick soup and brought a spoonful to Quinn's lips.

"Please," she begged, "try some soup. It will help you regain your strength."

He only shook his head, then turned his face from her.

Discouraged, Ashley set the tray on the table and rested back in the chair, watching his inert form. Heavy brooding silence filled the room, and from his post at the door, Gene shifted uncomfortably.

Ashley peered around at the slouched form. The dim light in the room seemed to accent his unusual pale eyes. They glowed in the dark like an animal's. Fatigue deepened the lines in his face and hunched his shoulders. Gene looked almost as pitiful as Quinn.

"I really don't believe it is necessary for you to remain," she said. "Mr. Jones is very ill and as the only person here with medical training, I feel I must stay by his bedside. I'm sure Mr. Oscar would sympathize with your need to rest. The last two days have been particularly exhausting for you."

Gene stared at the motionless figure under the sheets, shrugged, then shuffled into the room. He stopped first at the bureau, lit a lamp, then continued his inspection into drawers, cupboards, under and on top of all the furniture.

Her curiosity aroused, at last Ashley asked, "What are you looking for?"

"Guns, knives."

Covering her lips with cold fingertips, she stifled a gasp. "Really, Mr. Gene, you do me much more credit than I deserve. I wouldn't know what to do with such a weapon were I to locate one. And, as you can see, Mr. Jones is in no condition to move from the bed."

Gene stared at the pathetic form, nodded, gave the room one final scrutinizing look. Leaving the door wide open, he disappeared down the hall.

She gave a sigh of relief and settled back in the chair. In the unthreatening quiet, her nerves began to unknot and she relaxed. Idly, she watched Quinn's high-boned, red-bronzed face profiled in the lamplight. He was not a handsome man. Not in the way she had previously thought of handsome. Yet the strength of the wide jaw and square chin, the long, slightly crooked nose, all came together to make the kind of face she dreamed about.

Until this moment, she had found nothing lacking in him. He had displayed great courage in the face of terrible odds; he was polite, indicating a proper raising; his eye didn't wander over a woman leaving her feeling used. His character seemed above reproach, and she suspected he held a deep, personal faith in the Lord Jesus Christ.

But now he lay, the fight gone from him. His spirit seemed to have withdrawn, leaving a defeated, pain-wracked shell. He had given up when he needed to fight the hardest.

Time dragged as Ashley watched Quinn's regular breathing. Was the bump on his head more severe than she suspected? Were there internal injuries she couldn't treat? She fretted that somehow she had missed something.

Without turning his head toward her, he said something in a muffled voice.

She leaned forward to catch the words. Too late. He stopped talking. "I didn't hear what you said."

"Gene gone?" he repeated a bit louder.

"Yes. Has been for a long time."

Slowly, he turned to her and stretched. "Any chance for some food? I could eat boot leather without condiments."

"Wha . . ." she stammered. "You said you weren't hungry."

"Said I didn't feel like eating. Suddenly, I'm starved."

"You seem to tell all manner of half-truths," she lectured as she helped him to sit. "In fact, since we met yesterday morning, you have contrived several fabrications. It appears to me, you would be much better advised to try the truth. It might shock you to know that situations do get solved without resorting to such deviations." She placed the tray on his lap and stepped back.

For a moment Quinn studied her carefully, then without comment he began eating the cold soup.

"I must confess, though, I am relieved you're not too badly injured," Ashley said. "I was worried that I had made an error in estimating the seriousness of your wounds."

He grunted and clutched his chest.

"Mr. Jones!" Ashley gasped and knelt at the edge of the bed.

"Don't fret. Mighty sore in the midsection and a roaring headache, but I don't think it'll be fatal. I figure if they think I'm in a real bad way, maybe they'll get careless. Give us an opening." He looked at her with a shy smile. "How are the others doing?"

"Father seems all right. Pastor Grove and Mr. Sterling

didn't appear too happy when I last saw them."

He didn't look up from eating.

"Do you have a plan?"

"Not right now. Just have to keep our eyes open and watch," he said between bites. He wiped his mouth with the napkin, then handed her the tray.

He had left nothing, not one crumb. How was she going to explain the empty dishes to Gene without giving away Quinn's true condition? Then she wondered why she was even considering aiding Mr. Jones in his deception?

Before she could dispose of the tray, Ashley heard familiar shuffling footsteps coming down the hall. Quickly, she sat down on the edge of the bed and placed the tray on the table beside her as she tried to think of an acceptable explanation for the empty tray. The napkin was still in her hand as Gene appeared at the door.

"Big appetite for a skinny lady," Gene said, entering the room silently.

Startled at his words, Ashley looked up and with a dainty flip of the napkin, placed it on the empty dishes.

"I seen you eat downstairs and now you slicked up his tray." He stepped into the circle of light, and the small flame sent flickering shadows playing over his lined, dough-colored cheeks. "You'd be a hard woman to keep around. Take most of a working man's pay each day to keep ya fed and still you'd stay scrawny as an old hen."

He shrugged. "Don't matter none to me if you eat more'n two people, just so long as you don't give me no trouble." He stepped nearer the bed and looked carefully at Quinn. Having satisfied himself that Quinn was still no threat, Gene ordered, "Take the tray downstairs, then get back up here."

Glancing at Quinn, she saw he was sprawled in much the same position as when Gene appeared—his face averted, appearing pitifully helpless. "I'll return in a moment," she said as she stood.

131

He did not answer.

She was about mid-way down the stairs when the door into the study opened, and Oscar ushered the somber group of prisoners at gunpoint into the foyer.

With unreadable eyes, Oscar watched her descend the last few steps to the entrance way. "How is your husband doing?" he asked. His voice held no warmth or caring.

Oscar doesn't care how Mr. Jones is as long as he doesn't die before they locate the gold. She opened her mouth to tell him as much but Gene didn't give her a chance to speak.

"Not real good," he answered for her.

"That right?" Oscar asked Ashley.

She looked blankly at him.

"Be a shame if he were unable to move for a couple of days." Oscar turned to the other bandits. "Wouldn't it upset you boys if Mr. Jones couldn't get around for awhile?"

"Just as long as his tongue works and he tells us where that gold is, he can lie abed all he wants," Sidell said, chortling in evil delight.

A look of despair collected on the faces of the silent hostages. They turned and dragged up the stairs. Only the shuffling of their feet on the carpet broke the uneasy silence.

Chapter 11

Ashley delivered Quinn's supper tray to the kitchen, then returned upstairs. Quinn lay as she had left him, deep, regular breathing telling of his sound sleep.

As she moved a chair near the bed to take up her night watch, Jake and Davey, followed by Oscar, walked into the bedroom. Oscar crossed at once to the bed and studied Quinn's slack form. Then with the muzzle of his pistol, Oscar jabbed at Quinn. There was no reaction.

A look of surprise flicked over his face. "Jones is getting worse, isn't he?" Oscar turned to Ashley. "Well, you'd better see he doesn't die until he tells us where that gold room is."

Ashley flared, "I have done all I can. I want him alive, too, you know."

Oscar looked slightly abashed. "I guess you do, at that," he mumbled.

Davey, with the ever-present Hiller by his side, slowly walked to the bedside and stared at the unmoving figure.

The flickering lamplight accented his tightly drawn face. The sight tugged at Ashley's heart. *Poor little boy,* she thought, but there was no way she could reassure him without jeopardizing Quinn.

Jake moved inside the circle of light. "Boy looks real bad, doesn't he? Lots worse than when we pulled him up." Jake glanced at Oscar, now a rigid silhouette in the doorway. "Think it was the climb up the stairs that did it?" Jake asked Ashley.

Ashley pounced on his opening. "It most certainly could have. These men are so anxious to obtain the wealth they imagine is here, they'll kill one or all of us for it."

"A great waste of their time and our lives," Jake said easily. "But there's no dealing with crazy folk, especially them that's developed a severe case of gold fever." He shrugged and continued to stare at Quinn.

Suddenly, Ashley wanted very badly to see her father and be comforted.

Oscar shoved his gun in its holster. "You all stay in here and don't try anything fancy." He looked to include Jake in the warning. "The boys and I have some things to discuss. We'll be right outside in the hall." He stepped into the corridor and motioned to the men.

Ashley gathered Davey into the circle of her arms and held him close. Jake, his face a solemn mask, ambled to the window. Motioning Ashley to join him, he whispered, "Quinn looks like he's about done for. It ain't right for a strong man to go like that. Fallin' off a cliff 'cause some dumb cayuse get's a burr under his saddle. A dadburned useless way to ... " Jake choked and his voice trailed off.

The limp figure on the bed stirred. With a groan, Quinn turned over and grabbed his midsection. "Don't believe everything you see," he said softly.

The old man whirled about. Relief spread over his face, and he clutched the window sill for support. "Well, I'll be ... !" he exclaimed. "You sure had me fooled."

134

Quinn laid a finger over his lips. "Figured if the boys thought I was on my last legs, we could buy some time while we planned a way to distract them."

Their conversation halted abruptly as Oscar came into the room. "All right, Jake, you've had enough time with Jones. If he's as sick as he seems to be, any more talking will wear him right out. George is waiting to tuck you in bed." A slow, mirthless smile cut the harsh lines of his face.

"You don't mean he's going to sleep inside my room?" Jake snorted.

"Not hardly. In case he should doze off, don't want you knowing it so you can jump him. He'll be right outside in the hall. You'll never know who's awake and who isn't. Since the rooms are too high above the ground for a sane person to consider escaping that way, we can all sleep tonight."

Jake didn't look pleased with the arrangements, but he allowed himself to be led off without further objections.

Just before Oscar disappeared through the doorway, Ashley asked, "May I see my father before we settle for the night?"

Oscar considered her request. "Don't guess it'll hurt," he finally muttered. Folding his arms, he leaned against the door jamb and studied the limp figure on the bed. "He's not going anywhere."

Ashley studied Quinn for some moments, then turned to reassure Davey. His frightened eyes were fixed on Quinn. She knelt before the little boy and smoothed his hair in gentle strokes. "Davey," she said softly, "Mr. Jones is going to be all right. You stay here and watch after him. I'll tuck you in bed as soon as I return." She felt his thin body melt against her, as little arms slipped around her neck. Ashley thought she would melt from the reaction she experienced at his embrace.

Picking Davey up, she carried him to the sofa. Removing his shoes, she tucked a robe around him. Then, without a

135

glance at Oscar, Ashley swept from the room and down the hall.

All the bedroom doors stood open and, against each door frame, a guard lounged. Their faces, haggard from lack of sleep, looked grey in the soft lamplight glowing from the wall sconces.

Sidell slumped against the wall and Ashley said, "Mr. Sidell, you look worn out. I do hope you'll be able to get some rest tonight."

Slowly, red-rimmed eyes focused on her, and he scratched at the thin blue scar that stood like a brand on his lined face. "Not likely," he growled. "Not unless we tie everyone up, and Oscar won't hear of that." He cast an angry look down the hallway at Oscar who guarded the stairs.

That's strange, Ashley thought. She hadn't given Oscar credit for such an act of kindness. "What is his objection to binding us?"

"Says that'll make all of you stay awake working to get untied." His voice filled with disgust at the mention of Oscar's prediction.

Grudgingly, Ashley acknowledged that Oscar was probably right.

As she neared her father's room, George's darting eyes fixed on her, and his palm slipped over the handle of his pistol. His act drew her attention to the others' guns. They were all holstered. Now that Oscar thought Quinn was no threat, the bandit really was planning a peaceful night.

Smiling at George, she said, "Mr. Oscar said I might look in on my father."

George tipped his head to indicate it was safe to enter. However, his hand continued to rest on the pistol.

"Pastor Grove, Mr. Sterling, Father," she greeted the three men sharing the room, forcing a light tone to her voice. Pastor Grove, stretched out on one of the two beds in the room, his head propped with pillows, looked up from his Bible reading and attempted to focus weak grey

136

eyes on her. He smiled a greeting, and returned his attention to the worn book in his hand.

Mr. Sterling, once again hugging the mysterious satchel to his body, sat stiffly in a straightbacked chair near the window. Unnaturally bright eyes peered from his fatigue-drawn face and darted between George and Ashley as she entered. He gave no recognition of her greeting, but his eyes never left her.

"I've come to see how you are feeling, Father."

"That's most thoughtful of you, Daughter. Particularly in light of your great concern for the condition of Mr. Jones. How is he doing?" Lord Peter's voice carried well into the hall.

"I regret to say that the future seems very uncertain." Ashley's voice trembled and reaching for a handkerchief, she held it to her mouth.

"There, there, my dear." Lord Peter patted her awkwardly on the back. "This is a difficult time. But be strong." He took her into his arms and continued patting her back as though burping her.

Surprised by her father's words, Ashley surrendered briefly to tears. At last, she stepped away, pocketed her handkerchief, and studied her father. Beyond looking a bit tired, he appeared in fine health. "You still haven't told me how you are feeling."

"I confess the pace and excitement of the past two days have been a bit hard on an old man." Lord Peter sank onto his half of the bed he would share with Pastor Gideon, and Ashley knelt to remove his shoes.

He asked in a murmur, "How is Quinn?"

"He's fine," she whispered.

Lord Peter nodded, his face a model of grave concern. "I see," he said.

Ashley lifted Lord Peter's feet onto the bed and bent to loosen his collar.

George sank onto the hall floor across from the bedroom door. They all watched until his head sagged

137

onto his chest, and heavy, ragged snores erupted with a comforting degree of regularity.

Mr. Sterling rose and faced Ashley. "I am a desperate man," he moaned softly. "I must be in Leadville tomorrow. I absolutely must be!" He hiccupped a distinct sob.

Ashley straightened from tending her father and examined the pitiful man. "Mr. Sterling, I don't know what I can do to help you." She towered over the weeping man, and this made the situation even more uncomfortable. "Mr. Sterling, you must stop crying. It only makes matters worse."

"I know," he agreed and swallowed against the sobs choking him.

"Here, let me help you to bed," Ashley offered. He permitted her to guide him to the unoccupied bed. "What is in Leadville that you must attend?" she asked as she turned back the covers.

"I'm a desperate man," he mumbled again and wiped the tears from his cheeks with the back of one hand. "I've done a terrible thing. I have fifty thousand dollars in this satchel."

Despite her practiced self-control, Ashley's knees buckled, and she dropped onto the bed. "You what?" she gasped.

"I know I'm a fool to bring that amount of cash this way, but I had no choice. I deal in real estate. Sometimes, when I can see a quick profit, I buy and sell mines. I have a daughter in Denver. She has portrayed herself as wealthy and next month she is planning to marry into one of Denver's finest families. I didn't know where I would get the money for the wedding until this opportunity came along. It was a godsend, but I *must,* absolutely *must,* be in Leadville tomorrow."

So that's why he was so eager to marry me, conditions and all.

Taking out a once-white handkerchief, Morton Sterling wiped away beads of sweat glistening on his bald head.

Then he continued. "I received a tip at the bank in Durango where I work. They said the owners of a rich mine in Leadville were in financial trouble and being forced to sell one mine to protect the rest of their properties. I did some investigating and found this to be true. A friend in Leadville sought out the mine owners and learned that if they could get their hands on fifty thousand dollars cash by tomorrow, they would take it and ask no questions."

Mr. Sterling's hands wrapped and unwrapped themselves around the handles of the black bag, growing more frenzied in their movements as he talked. "I have mortgaged my house, my daughter's jewelry, all my property. If I lose out and don't make the deal, I'm a ruined man," he whimpered. "But if I succeed, I'll double my money and have my daughter married to a man who can keep her in the style she desires."

A shadow loomed across the room. Ashley raised her eyes and froze. The muzzle of a gun barrel pointed straight at her.

George scowled. "You been talkin' long enough."

Ashley managed a nod and pushed herself to her feet. "I'll prepare you a glass of soda water, Mr. Sterling. That should help you sleep."

Blotting at his damp face, Morton Sterling managed a sick smile. "That will be most appreciated," he murmured.

Ashley pushed past George and hurried to her room. Returning with a small box of bicarbonate of soda, she prepared the drink for Mr. Sterling. Satisfied that all was innocent, George resumed his position in the hallway.

Ashley moved to her father's bedside. As she bent to fluff his pillows, he grasped her arm and pulled her down. Whispering, he said, "We obviously are going to be delayed in our journey. There is no guarantee that we will reach Cheyenne in time for you to choose a husband." His eyes narrowed as he stared intently at her. "Therefore, you must select your future husband from the candidates available here in Harmer City."

"Father!" Ashley gasped. "You can't be serious."

"I have never been more serious in my life. So as you pray tonight, consider the possibilities. If you don't make a choice by one week from this Saturday, I shall choose for you."

"But what if your choice doesn't want me?" she forced herself to ask.

"From the available men, I'm sure I shall find one who will accept my offer."

"Your offer?"

"I shall offer the man a goodly sum of money to become your husband. There are enough greedy souls in this little town. I'm sure I shall have no trouble locating a mate for you. And thanks to the presence of Pastor Grove, we can even have a proper wedding."

Ashley studied her father's face. His eyes never wavered, and his mouth was drawn into a determined line.

"I shall make my considerations, Father," she said, "and let you know."

"I expected you would, Daughter." Lord Peter shot her a penetrating look. "Blow out the lamp as you leave." He rolled onto his side, and Ashley found herself staring at his broad back.

When Ashley entered her bedroom, the lamp was out. Quinn and Davey were sleeping soundly. Quickly she removed her shoes and stretched out on the edge of Davey's sofa bed. Though her body surrendered to the luxury of the soft couch, her mind took no notice of it. The ultimatum forced on Ashley by Lord Peter spun through her head as she lay staring into the half-darkness. Quinn was definitely a man she could marry, but beyond treating her with respect, he had given no indication he desired to become more than a casual acquaintance. She would not lower herself to play coy games with him in the hope of changing his mind.

These disquieting thoughts tumbled through her mind

140

until, at last, exhaustion produced a troubled sleep. Ashley dreamed she, not Quinn, fell over the edge of the trail. No ledge caught her, and she plummeted into the gorge below. Miraculously, she wasn't killed, but no one wanted to attempt her rescue. Lord Peter pleaded with all the men, offering them great sums of money. They laughed at him, saying that with a room of gold awaiting them, money was hardly a worthy bribe.

At last, he said the man who saved her could have her hand in marriage and that drew even more laughter. Their great howls of merriment became fainter as the mule train moved on up the canyon. At last, only the rush of the stream broke the silence.

Rocks clinked near her and she looked up to see Lord Peter leaning out over the rim of the trail.

"Goodbye, Daughter," he called. "I guess you should have married when you had the chance. Now, with you dead, I inherit all the money."

Ashley woke in a cold sweat, her heart pounding, and her cheeks wet with tears. Restless from her nightmare, she slipped off the couch and tiptoed to the window. Outside, it had started snowing again, heavily. Her heart dropped into the pit of her stomach. They could be snowed in here until spring.

"You plannin' to jump, or somethin'?" Gene growled. Ashley started.

She turned to face him. His pistol was aimed at her heart. "N..n..no." She pointed as she stepped back from the window. "See."

Gene looked outside at the large swirling flakes. Ashley could almost hear the cogs go round inside his head. "Don't look good," he said, at last. "Don't look good at all. I'd better tell Oscar." Gene hurried from the room, and soon Ashley could hear the bandits conferring.

"What's happening?" Sidell asked.

"It's snowin' hard. Real hard," Gene said. "We ain't gonna get out with that gold if we don't get a move on.

Might be here all winter."

"What do you say, George?" Oscar asked. "You're the one who knows this country."

"I'm fer waitin' a few days. This is the first storm of the season. Always clears up fer a spell afterwards. If what we've heard is true, we could get us a good haul to add to what we got offen that train. Pure gold's worth a little inconvenience."

Oscar nodded. "I'm not inclined to agree with you, George. But as long as we got plenty of food and a comfortable place to bunk, we'd be fools to let this opportunity slip away. We'll stay a few days."

Ashley's heart sank. She and Lord Peter were never going to get to Cheyenne in time. She would have to marry someone in Harmer City.

Lord, I don't understand why you have done this to me. Whenever I've prayed about this, you've always led me to believe the right man was out there if I would be faithful to your command. I've kept my faith, Lord. I've kept to your Word. Her chin trembled as she fought back the tears. With her body and mind exhausted from the trials of the past two days, however, Ashley had no success. Scalding tears squeezed from under closed eyelids, and a painful sob constricted her chest.

Chapter 12

In the days that followed, the weather did not clear as George had predicted. Though it stopped snowing, a heavy fog settled in and refused to lift. Everything was shrouded in a dense white blanket that blended with the snow until it was impossible to define any features.

Ashley occupied her time by nursing Quinn. By the third day, he had to get out of bed. This allowed her more time to read, play with Davey, and think up excuses to stay out of her father's way.

She and Quinn were never alone long enough to discuss anything personal. As though reading her mind, however, he had made several general statements about his intentions never to marry. He apologized for placing her in the circumstance of appearing to be his wife and assured her the charade would end as soon as he could concoct a safe plan to remove the robbers.

The fifth day of their captivity dawned in the same gloomy way as the preceding days. The prisoners, including Quinn, were assembled for breakfast. Oscar looked out the dining room window and observed in disgust as he had each morning, "Can't travel in this stuff. Can't even find our way to the mine. We wouldn't dare try to move on to the Utah territory. Get ourselves killed falling down a crevasse."

"Wouldn't that be a shame," Sidell snarled.

Litch stepped forward and fixed his pistol on Oscar. George aimed his revolver at Litch.

Oscar looked with tired disgust at the man. "Stop playing games. Put those guns on the people who need guarding!"

The tension between the outlaws was growing, and Ashley wondered how much longer Oscar could keep them under control. The weather, their cross purposes, and mutual distrust were taking a heavy toll on their dispositions and common sense.

Molly came into the room carrying a large kettle. With a grim look set on her face, she started slapping a heaping spoonful of sticky mush into each person's bowl. When the last portion was served, she marched up to Oscar. "You'd better do something soon, mister. I don't have enough supplies to keep feeding three meals a day to a mob that eats like this bunch."

Litch leaped to his feet, overturning his chair and sending it crashing to the floor. "Ya callin' us pigs, woman?" he shouted.

Ashley observed a fleeting look of uncertainty cross Oscar's face. "All right, everyone," he snapped. "Stay as you are and *don't* move beyond eating. Sit down, Litch. George, keep them in line while the rest of us have a little talk." He motioned the outlaws out into the foyer.

A short time later the men returned. Oscar pointed his pistol at Quinn. "Jones, get out here."

Quinn quirked an eyebrow, shoved his chair from the table, and sauntered into the foyer. Gene appeared behind Ashley and motioned for her to follow.

In the entrance hall, Gene kept two pistols aimed at them while Oscar faced Quinn toward the wall and bound his hands behind his back. Then he whirled Ashley into the same position. Stunned by such unexpected treatment, she submitted meekly as he grabbed her right wrist and crossed it over her left. She could feel the thin rope bite into her skin as he trussed her hands.

Oscar pulled Quinn away from the wall and shoved him toward the stairs. Quinn staggered and nearly fell. Gene grasped a handful of Ashley's hair and pulled her into the middle of the hallway. She felt the hard point of a gun barrel ram into the middle of her back, and a small gasp escaped before she could clamp her jaws together. Were they going to shoot her and Quinn?

"All right, you two, up the stairs," Oscar ordered.

Quinn didn't move. "Why?" he demanded.

"Shut up," Oscar snarled, giving the ropes an impatient tug. "Just do what I tell you."

Oscar and Gene escorted Quinn and Ashley up the stairs and into Quinn's bedroom. Oscar stepped to the window and looked out. It was a long drop to the ground. "Hope you try to climb out," he said to Quinn as he checked his bonds. "Be a good way to break your neck, and we'd be rid of you."

Quinn regarded Oscar with unfathomable eyes and stoic face.

Oscar inspected George's work on Ashley's ropes. "Sit!" he ordered, indicating two chairs at the dressing table.

Quinn, glaring his anger, wrestled his way from Gene's grasp. Oscar whipped his pistol barrel to Ashley's temple. "Go on, ugly. Fight! See what happens to your lovely wife."

Quinn's shoulders slumped, and reluctantly he let his long, lean frame settle onto the chair. Oscar moved the other chair across the room from Quinn, guided Ashley to it, and shoved her down. Then, while Oscar held the gun, Gene, with practiced ease, tied Quinn and Ashley securely

145

to the chairs.

"You two better sit quiet," Oscar warned. "Remember, we still have Jake . . . and Davey."

The color drained from Quinn's face, but his eyes narrowed with anger.

"We'll be downstairs, right under this room," Oscar reminded them. "Any time you move, we'll hear it."

Gene and Oscar backed out into the hallway and locked the door.

"Oh, Mr. Jones," Ashley wailed softly. "What are we to do?"

"We are going to do exactly as the man says. Stay absolutely still and listen. Maybe we can piece together what they're up to."

"This house is so soundproof, with the door closed we can't even hear them going down the stairs."

"Nevertheless, at this point, we can't make any trouble. Oscar is angry enough to be extremely dangerous."

They sat for what seemed hours, listening intently. Their tall bodies cramped painfully on the chairs. Each time either one shifted, the wooden joints squeaked a protest, shattering the heavy quiet.

Other than the occasional creak, the silent hours dragged by with no sounds from the interior of the house.

After awhile Ashley dozed. When she woke, sunshine was streaming into the room. "Mr. Jones," she whispered. "The fog has lifted."

"I know. I've been awake for quite awhile."

"I thought surely Oscar would be back by now," Ashley said.

"Maybe there are problems downstairs. Jake's not one to surrender what's his without a fight, and I get the distinct feeling your father's a fighter, too. Maybe they've hatched up something. It's been too quiet for too long. I don't think they're still in the house."

She permitted herself to raise her eyes and met his

146

unwavering gaze. The harsh shadows cast by the sunbeams accented the rough-hewn planes of his face. He really was a most extraordinary man.

Unblinking, Quinn returned her gaze, squinting his eyes as if he were having difficulty focusing. As the moments lingered, the hard years began rolling from him, and he looked surprisingly young and vulnerable. Something pulled at her heart as his dark, penetrating eyes searched her face.

He ordered, "Turn your chair around. I'm coming over to untie your hands."

Ashley turned her back to Quinn while he scooted his chair toward hers until their hands touched. When he paused to catch his breath and to listen, Ashley said, "I shall set you free first. Then, if someone should come, you'll be able to disarm him."

Every creak of the building startled her and kept her heart racing. But no one came. She fumbled with Quinn's rope, only partially able to feel the strong knots with her numbed fingertips. Though she pulled and tugged, it seemed an eternity before the knot loosened and the rope fell away.

Quinn rubbed the circulation back into his hands, then unfastened her hands.

"Oh, my, but that does feel wonderful!" she exclaimed softly.

"It won't feel so wonderful when the blood starts making your hands tingle," he said. "Can get pretty painful."

"Sounds like this has happened to you before," Ashley commented. She stood and spread her cold palms to the heat of the sun.

He smiled ruefully. "I seem to have a knack for attracting trouble." He joined her in the sunlight. "If I were *sure* the house was empty, I'd break down the door," he said.

They both turned to look at the heavy slab door

147

anchored with heavy iron hinges.

"Please don't try," Ashley said. "Your ribs may feel better, but they're not ready to serve as a battering ram against anything that sturdy."

Quinn fingered his still bound ribs and nodded his agreement.

Ashley looked out the window at the deep drifts. "Are you snowed in here all winter?"

"We are."

"What happens if someone gets sick? Really sick or injured?"

Quinn shrugged. "They get well or they die."

"How can you be so calm about such matters?"

"When a person decides to live up here, those are some of the risks he accepts."

"Don't you care if you live or die?"

"I care very much, but what is living for one person is merely existing for another. I'm willing to accept the risks for the freedom and stimulation."

Ashley pondered his words. The more she knew about him, the less she understood. Here was a man who wanted nothing more from life than to live in the rarefied atmosphere of a high mountain valley and act as bodyguard to a wealthy mine owner. When this mine was played out, he undoubtedly would move on to another, and another, dragging that poor little boy from one mining camp to another. Such a way of life was unfathomable to Ashley, and yet her father was going to make her choose a husband from among men for whom no other kind of life was acceptable. Her shoulders sagged and a deep sigh escaped.

"Please have faith for a bit longer. I'm sure this is all going to work out for the best," he said, misreading her actions. Sitting on the couch, Quinn sprawled back, stretched out his long legs, and crossed his boots at the ankles.

She had the feeling, though, that he wasn't nearly as

relaxed as he appeared.

A key rattled in the lock. Ashley's heart leaped into her throat as Quinn sprinted to a position for attack. There was no time to replace the chairs where they had been, nor to pretend they were still tied. The rasp of metal against metal, the click as the lock opened, the clink as the knob turned kept Ashley breathless. The heavy slab door swung open and Sidell stood in the doorway.

"Why, Sidell, Oscar let you out to play?" Quinn taunted, relieved that it was not Oscar who had come.

"Watch yer mouth, big man," Sidell snarled. He brandished a gun but stayed in the doorway, a safe distance from Quinn. "Oscar's gone, fer yer information."

Quinn's mouth dropped at the news. "Gone! Where? Why?"

"Boys decided they'd had enough Colorado winter. Decided they'd best get out while the weather held and the gettin' was good. Lit out fer Utah. Some place called Corinne. Got relatives there. Ask me what I think? They was cowards. That's what they was. Big, braggin' cowards!"

"Not hardly," Quinn said softly.

"Oscar said me and Litch dreamed up the gold room. Said he'd had a belly full a-waitin' around fer it to turn up. Said they didn't need the money nohow. Had their saddlebags full a-money and gold from a big train robbery they pulled up Colorado Springs way."

The muscles along Quinn's jaw worked, and his eyes narrowed. "Where is everyone?"

"Me and Litch got the rest of the folks tied up in the Sally Forth. Don't think about tryin' to jump me. If I ain't back real soon, Litch's gonna start shootin' people."

Quinn took a step toward Sidell.

"Don't do somethin' dumb. Unless you want yer missus shot up. Won't kill her. Just hurt her some." Sidell clicked back the hammer and aimed at Ashley.

"Sidell! Take that weapon off her," Quinn shouted. "Now!"

"Big man, ya ain't in no position to give orders. Shut up and don't give me no more trouble." Sidell walked over to Ashley and whirled her around to face Quinn. "Take a good look at her. We're gonna shoot someone every hour until either you or Harmer decides to tell us where that gold room is. Every time we shoot someone, we'll put another bullet in her, too."

"Why, you cowardly skunk!" Quinn exploded. "You aren't man enough to stand up to me or Jake. You have to hide behind women and children."

"You cain't make me mad, Jones. Leastways, not until I get that gold. Then, my temper's liable to become uncontrollable."

Ashley felt her mouth grow dry. She knew he was threatening them all with death as soon as he had the gold.

Sidell motioned with his gun. "All right, let's go."

Ashley and Quinn stepped into the hall and walked quickly down the stairs. "Get yer coats on. Don't want ya freezin' afore ya tell me where ta find the gold."

Once outside, Ashley was surprised at how warm it was. She raised her hands to protect her eyes from sunlight reflected off the rapidly melting snow.

"Indian summer's back," Quinn said, squinting against the brightness. "Give this warm wind and the sun a few more hours, and most of the snow will be just a mushy memory for awhile."

"If you two don't get a move on, you won't be around to enjoy the weather."

"Where do you want us to go?" Quinn asked innocently.

"The Sally Forth, ya dumb biscuit. That's where the gold is."

"Well, if you know where it is, what do you need me for?"

"Because, I only know which mine it's in. I don't know where it is inside."

"Why don't you just look?"

"Yeah, why don't I? That mine's only got about fourteen big tunnels, and I don't know how many side shafts. I don't plan to make it a life's work findin' that strike."

Ashley felt the hard nose of Sidell's pistol in her back. "Any more talk from you, Jones, the lady here gets her first shot."

"Sidell, you aren't going to harm her anymore than you're going to kill me. You're dumb, but not dumb enough to hurt your two top hostages. Now take that gun out of my wife's back and stop scaring her to pieces."

Sidell looked slightly abashed at Quinn's tone of voice, but he stepped behind Ashley where he could keep a gun on them both, and allowed Quinn to lead the way to the mine.

Chapter 13

The sun had made the snow slushy and slick. Quinn stepped onto the path and slipped. Attempting to catch his balance, he took several reeling steps in Sidell's direction.

Sidell leaped back onto the veranda, dragging Ashley with him. "Jones!" he shouted. "Any more funny moves and yer missus gets it." He ground his gun into Ashley's ribs. "Lead out. Now!"

"Sidell, you ... you scum!" Quinn shouted back. His eyes glittered, hard and cold as ice.

Sidell's answer was to jab Ashley even harder and breathe a string of oathes at Quinn.

Ashley ignored the crude robber as he propelled her forward by the arm. She walked with as much dignity as the mushy path permitted.

Away from the house the trail narrowed and the climb grew steeper. She kept stepping on her dragging skirts and slipping. Gasping for breath, Ashley stumbled to a halt. "Mr. Sidell, my skirts are so heavy with water I can scarcely move. Please allow me to wring them out."

"Not on yer life," Sidell snapped. "Get along and don't be stoppin' fer every little thing." He bored into her back with his pistol.

"Sidell, get that gun off her and keep it off," Quinn commanded. "She's not a mountain goat like the rest of us. She needs to rest."

Sidell's eyes narrowed, and he sent a hate-filled look at Quinn. "She's rested long enough. Move and keep moving!" His impatience showed in his nervous thrusts of the pistol as he held it on them. He glared at Ashley. "You, I don't need! You're becoming a big nuisance. Don't stop again or I'll plug you."

Quinn whirled and looked down on Sidell. "Her, you do need. I'll never tell you where that room is if you make another threat to Lady Ashley or harm her in any way."

Sidell shouted, "Move!"

Under Sidell's gun they scrambled the final distance to a small, solidly built structure. Once inside, however, Ashley realized the shack was not a building after all. The stout little building only covered the mine shaft blasted into the rock of the mountainside.

The effort of blasting showed in the size of the entrance, narrow and so low both Ashley and Quinn had to duck to get into the mine tunnel. Ashley found herself staring into unrelieved blackness, unable to see Quinn stop in front of her. "Mr. Jones?" she said in a quaking voice.

"Right here," he said as she ran into him.

"Oh, do excuse me. I can't see a thing."

Quinn glowered at Sidell standing in the entrance and blocking most of the light. "If Sidell had good sense, he'd pick up a lantern from the stack there, and light it. While it's impossible to get lost in the main shaft, it's more reassuring to have some light."

"You'd like me to turn around, wouldn't ya? So's ya could jump me," Sidell snarled. "Nice work, Jones, but I ain't fallin' fer that old trick."

"Then let Mrs. Jones get the light. I doubt she has such evil thoughts."

Sidell looked uncertain, cleared his throat, and said, "All right, but don't ya make no false moves."

"I don't know what moves are false," Ashley said, all her fright showing.

"Them's the ones that look like yer tryin' somethin'."

"Mr. Sidell, I haven't the faintest notion what you are referring to. I would be happy to get a lantern, and light it so we can see. That is, I will if you'll step out of the entrance so I might pass."

"You'd like that, wouldn't ya? Then ya could knock the gun outta my hand. No, you'll both come back into the shanty while the lady lights the lantern. I'll carry it."

Sidell stepped into the little room, and Ashley and Quinn joined him there. Locating a lamp with a full well of oil, she fumbled her way through the lighting of the battered tin lantern.

"Now step lively into that shaft," Sidell ordered.

When Quinn and Ashley were far enough ahead to suit him, Sidell lifted the lantern up so they could see into the mine shaft. "Now, I've had enough shilly-shallyin' around. Get a move on er Litch is gonna get nervous. That ain't healthy fer them what's under his gun."

Through the grotesque shadows leaping over the pitted walls of the tunnel, they picked their way until the shaft curved in front of them. On the other side of the turn, the tunnel widened into a rock-walled vault hacked out of the solid stone. Heavy canvas bags stacked along the wall took up most of the limited space. A shadowy yellow glow from oil lamps showed the prisoners, gagged, bound hand and foot, and huddled close together under the low ceiling.

At the sight of Ashley and Quinn, the hostages' drawn faces lit. The hope she saw there made Ashley ill. She and Quinn were as helpless as they were. Suddenly, she

154

realized someone was missing. She whirled on Sidell and demanded, "Where's Davey?"

"Left the dumb kid and dog back at the house. Locked 'em in a room. Got enough security right here," Sidell growled. He turned to Litch. "Get anyone to talk?" he asked as he herded Ashley and Quinn across the cave.

Litch shook his head. A dark scowl shadowed his coarse greasy features, and he palmed his gun back and forth between his hands.

"No, Litch, yer not goin' to start shootin' just yet. We're gonna give old Jones here just a little bit more time to tell us where that vug is," Sidell said in the sweetest voice Ashley had heard him use.

"Have you truly found such a room?" Ashley asked Quinn.

"Sidell says I have," Quinn replied.

Sidell fumbled in his shirt pocket and produced a small chunk of raw gold. "I know yer have. I got this to prove it."

The small nugget of gold cradled in the palm of Sidell's hand sparkled in the dim lamp light, bearing witness to the truth of his declaration.

Ashley gasped. "A piece of raw gold that size would be worth . . . . "

"A pretty penny," Sidell finished for her. "Too bad you ain't gonna get any."

So there really was a golden room! Ashley shivered when she looked at the greed spewing from the eyes of Sidell and Litch. Any hope that they might survive this ordeal died.

Quinn's eyes turned as cold and hard as the gold nugget in Sidell's hand. "Where'd you get that?" His voice splintered the air like chips of ice.

"Wouldn't you like to know?" Sidell taunted.

Quinn's eyes bored into the scarred face. "Yes, I would. And you're going to tell me." He took a step toward Sidell and a shimmer of lamplight caught Litch's pistol as he raised it at Quinn.

"Go ahead. Shoot! Then you'll never know where the gold is." Now it was Quinn's turn to taunt.

"You admit you got a gold room!" Sidell shouted and a coarse, dry laugh spilled from his chapped lips.

"I admit nothing. I'm only saying that if you shoot me, you'll never know."

As he thought, Sidell scratched the blue scar where it entered the wiry beard. Finally he said, "I guess it can't hurt none to tell ya." He settled on an ore sack and looked at Quinn. "After that frakus Litch had with ya in Denver, we followed ya until we knowed where ya hailed from. We was ridin' the high country here, lookin' fer a way to get even when we happened on a bunch of Injuns. Same tribe as that squaw, Morning Star. They was passin' around this here piece of gold, excited and blubberin' about how it come from a gold room here at the Sally Forth mine."

"Indians!" Quinn sneered. "Even as dumb as you are, Sidell, you can create a better story than that."

Sidell's mouth curled, and his finger worked on and off the trigger of his gun. "It's gonna be a real pleasure to pump a bullet . . . . "

"Don't you think I know you're going to kill us, anyway?" Quinn said quietly. "That's why I won't tell you anything. Ever!"

Sidell let out a roar, grabbed Ashley around the waist and crushed her against his chest. Jamming his revolver into her temple, he glared at Quinn. "Ya want yer bride alive, you'll tell me." His gravelly voice shook with his anger.

Quinn replied by folding his arms and leaning against the pitted wall of the cold room. He fixed Sidell with slitted eyes, opaque and hard. Ashley could not control the shiver that wracked her body. *Oh, dear Lord, if you have chosen this way for my death, help me to die with dignity,* she pleaded. She felt strength and calm flow through her, and suddenly she no longer feared either

Litch or Sidell. Straightening to her full height, Ashley looked down on the stocky figure holding her.

"Mr. Sidell, if you please. You are crushing the breath from me," she said in a wheezing whisper. "If you don't release your grip, very soon I shall not be a worthy hostage."

"I ain't lettin' ya go, Missus Jones, so ye better learn to get along on what air yer gittin'."

Her vision fogged and, though she fought against it, her knees turned limber. She swayed. This forced Sidell to hold her up.

"Sidell!" Quinn snapped. "Let her go! I'm not telling you a thing even if you shoot her."

At Quinn's words her heart stopped, fluttered a few weak beats like the wings of an indecisive butterfly, then sank like a lead weight into the pit of her stomach. Ashley moaned and sagged her full weight against Sidell. The click of the gun echoed in her ears as he pulled the hammer back.

She closed her eyes and began repeating the Lord's Prayer. The pressure of the gun made her head hurt. Suddenly, she wished Sidell would conclude her execution.

"Ya got one more chance to change yer mind" Sidell growled at Quinn.

"Sidell," Quinn said, "we're all dead people whether you get the gold or not. We know that. I'd sooner be dead without your growing rich over it."

The look he flashed Ashley was brief, but in the depths of his eyes she read his agony. *Oh, praise the Lord,* her heart sang. *Mr. Jones does care. He might even love me.* With this knowledge she straightened, holding her head high and letting her eyes rest on Quinn.

The gun at her temple twisted as though trying to bore into her brain.

"I'm a-gonna do it," Sidell warned again.

Still relaxed and looking almost amiable, Quinn smiled

slightly and said, "I know you are and so does she. Why don't you get it over with?"

Sidell's feet shuffled against the rocky floor as though he were bracing himself for the kill. The scraping sound of his feet echoed hollowly through the chamber. Ashley's eyes linked with Quinn's for a brief moment. Then, taking a deep breath, she closed her eyes and concentrated on the placement of the gun barrel. The pressure produced an ever increasing ache in her temple. The pain seeped into her brain. Surely the explosion would come any second. She clenched her hands against the inevitable.

And still he didn't shoot.

"Please, Mr. Sidell. Please get it over with," Ashley pleaded.

The gun barrel jabbed harder. Sidell cleared his throat. His breath quickened.

This is it! Ashley steeled herself.

Nothing happened!

Then, without warning, the pressure left her temple, and Sidell's arm released its grip.

Ashley's eyes flew open, and her heart stopped. There, filling the shadowy darkness of the cave-like room stood a dozen silent, grim Indians. Their faces were painted with grotesque designs. In their hands they gripped rifles, knives, and bows. Ashley felt the blood rush from her head, and she swayed on unsteady legs.

Sidell and Litch had wilted in surprise at the number of armed Indians. One Indian moved forward to bind the two men and place gags in their mouths.

A handsome warrior stepped out of the mouth of the tunnel and stood surveying the scene. He motioned, and two Indians took up positions on either side of Quinn. Then the warrior turned and nodded. Morning Star stepped into the room.

A look of confusion passed over the prisoners' faces.

"What's the meaning of this, Morning Star?" Quinn protested.

Morning Star glanced at Quinn without speaking, then turned to the tall warrior by her side. "Are we ready, Red Fox?" she asked.

He nodded.

"Very well. Mr. Jones, we are waiting to be shown the golden room."

"Morning Star, I asked you before, what do you think you are doing?" Quinn repeated his question.

Morning Star stepped up beside Quinn. "My people once hunted and fished this land. Until the white man cheated us of our heritage, this belonged to us. Now, we are being sent away to a reservation. Denied that which is rightfully ours. We have little money, and this room of gold will help provide for us in our new land. We are obviously not equipped for rigorous mining. We will take only what we can carry in the bags we have brought with us."

Quinn interrupted Morning Star. "Tell me how you learned of the vug. Only four people knew of its existence. I didn't tell and neither did Jake. I can't believe the other two men did either."

"Your mine security chief and the superintendent didn't knowingly tell. They were up on the mountain one day talking about the discovery. Some of my people were hunting nearby and overheard the conversation. We have waited long and patiently for the right time to take what is ours." Morning Star cast a disgusted look at Sidell and Litch. Securely bound, they cowered on the damp, rocky floor. "Everything was going well until those two muddled in. We could even have managed with them, but Oscar and his men made things too risky. There was nothing to do but wait and watch again."

Red Fox stalked over to Quinn. "Enough talk!" He gave Quinn a shove toward the large tunnel leading out of the room and deeper into the mountain. "Now it is time to see this room of gold."

Morning Star nodded and picked up a lantern, moving forward through the shaft. Quinn, forced at knife point by

Red Fox, ducked into the low, narrow tunnel. Indian warriors each claimed a prisoner and followed Red Fox.

Ashley's heart stopped, then beat in wild, unrhythmic flutterings as her guard unsheathed his knife. He pressed the glittering blade into her back. He grunted something she didn't understand and shoved her after Quinn. Nearly blind with terror, she stumbled forward into the feebly lighted slit blasted into the mountain of rock.

Chapter 14

The tunnel's low ceiling forced the captives and their guards to crouch nearly double as they shuffled forward in single file behind Morning Star and Quinn who led the way deep into the heart of the mountain. Her flickering miner's lantern cast grotesque shadows that slithered over the ceiling and walls of the narrow shaft.

Footfalls on the loose rock layering the man-made tunnel sent harsh chinking echoes through the passageway. When the party stopped to rest, the only sound beyond their heavy breathing was the erratic plink of water seeping through the ceiling and dripping onto the rocks below.

Gradually the shaft grew wider and higher until even Quinn, the tallest person, was able to stand upright.

Moving on, they wound from shaft to shaft until Ashley wondered how anyone could keep the directions straight.

"Are you sure you're leading us to the golden room or taking us on a wild goose chase?" Morning Star asked as they paused yet again to rest.

"I am not foolish enough to anger you or your people in such close quarters," Quinn replied.

After what seemed an eternity in the flickering darkness, the shaft took a sharp turn and Morning Star stopped before a recently erected barrier. She held up her lantern, and it illuminated a heavy slab door. The lumber still glowed the creamy yellow of new wood. An iron hasp and lock held a thick metal bolt in place.

Turning to face Quinn, Morning Star asked, "We have reached the room?"

Quinn looked back over his shoulder at Jake and cocked a quizzical eyebrow.

"That's right," Jake said. "Bolt on the door's heavy, though. You'll need help to lift it once it's unlocked." Slowly, Jake's eyes lifted to meet Quinn's impassive stare. "Give Morning Star the key, my boy."

Quinn turned to Red Fox who kept his knife point leveled at Quinn's throat. A dark scowl settled on the Indian's face as Quinn bent and produced a bright brass key from the heel of his left boot. Red Fox snatched the key from Quinn's fingers and handed it to Morning Star. She set down her lantern and fit the key into the lock. The click reverberated shot-like through the tunnel.

Red Fox helped Morning Star lift the bolt. Then, straining against unoiled hinges which stubbornly protested, Red Fox swung the door open.

Raising her lantern, Morning Star, with Red Fox and Quinn at her heels, stepped into a shimmering wonderland of pure gold. The other Indians urged the rest of the party inside the large room. Gasps of wonder rose from the group.

King Solomon with all his wealth had nothing to equal this, Ashley thought as she stood, open-mouthed, examining the vug. The room was probably twenty feet long, fifteen feet wide, and at least forty feet high. Glittering crystals of pure gold covered its walls and ceiling.

With trembling fingers, Morning Star reached out and plucked a crystal as big as Quinn's thumbnail. She rolled it into a maleable ball similar to the one Sidell had shown them earlier.

Sidell was the first to recover his voice. "See!" he bawled, his eyes hard with greed. "I told ya there was gold here!"

Looking scornfully at the slavering man, Quinn said, "Oh, there's gold here, right enough. Lots of it. And, Sidell, all you have to do is scrape it off the rocks. It's so pure it doesn't even have to be refined."

Quivering with avarice, Sidell stumbled to the nearest wall. With his hands bound tightly behind his back, he couldn't touch the gold. In a desperate attempt to feel the treasure, Sidell closed his eyes and rubbed his whiskered cheek slowly back and forth against the golden surface, moaning all the while, "I knowed it was here. I knowed it all the time. I can't ask for more in life than this." He wept with frustration. "If I can't have some of this wealth, let me die right here." Despair overcame him, and Sidell sank in a bawling, shapeless heap on the floor.

Litch watched Sidell without a flicker of emotion. His eyes, hard and beady, narrowed and rested briefly on the older man sobbing his disappointment. No one else paid the slightest attention to Sidell. Everyone, including the normally stoic Indians, stood thunderstruck, disbelief etching their faces.

At last Red Fox recovered and said, "This is truly as the white men said it was." He spoke in soft, reverent tones as he dropped some of the shiny crystals into the palm of his hand. "The Great Spirit has led us to this wealth to help our people. We must have all of it!"

At his words Quinn straightened ominously, and Lord Peter, who had remained unnaturally silent, came to life. "It does seem to me, Red Fox, that your people owe Mr. Harmer a considerable debt since without him you would never have had any gold. A great deal of work and expense went into uncovering this magnificent find."

The room grew quiet as Red Fox held his lantern in Lord Peter's face, studying it intently. At last, he said, "Spoken like a great chief, but one who does not know how we have been betrayed, robbed of our heritage by the greed of the white man, sent to live on worthless land he can see no use for. And, if the white man finds riches there, he will once more cheat us of that land and send us, broken and penniless, farther into the wilderness."

"But if such treatment is to stop, someone must begin." Lord Peter persisted. "You must honor Morning Star's assurances."

Red Fox looked with stern eyes at Lord Peter. "I will think on what you have said. So will my people."

"You know he's right, Red Fox," Quinn said.

All eyes turned toward the tall, angular figure.

"You never would have found this gold. It took bags of money and years of work, knowledge, and experience to get here."

"And no small amount of divine providence," Jake added.

A quick grin lifted the corner of Quinn's mouth. "Yes, a lot of that," he acknowledged.

Suddenly, Morton Sterling said, "There's enough gold here to share with everyone." As his eyes traveled over the room, his face glowed.

"How much do you think the gold in here is worth?" Morning Star asked.

Quinn furrowed his brow and scanned the room slowly and carefully. "As thick as the gold is layered, a rough guess says about two million dollars."

Cries of astonishment echoed through the room. Even Morning Star lost her cool detachment for a moment. She quickly recovered, however, and stared at Quinn with cold eyes.

"What say, Red Fox?" Quinn asked, "You willing to cut a deal?"

Red Fox, his face a mask and his eyes as unreadable as black onyx, looked first at Morning Star, then at Quinn. "I don't think so. No need to."

Quinn drew himself to full height and looked down on the stocky warrior. "There's plenty of need. Have you planned how you're going to get this gold out of here without the whole town knowing about it? Harmer City isn't a bad place, but it's a pretty typical mining town. We have plenty of rough characters here who'd also like a part of this gold. And they wouldn't be gentle in the taking."

The full effect of Quinn's words registered and Red Fox wavered. "Maybe we need to think a bit."

"Listen to the man, Red Fox," Jake said. "You know what he says is true. You not only won't get any gold, you stand a good chance of getting yourself and your people killed if the greed in Harmer City gets out of hand."

Quinn said, "Why do you think we kept this such a secret? We . . . Jake hasn't yet figured out the best way to mine it."

The shadows moved and Pastor Grove stepped away from his guard to face Red Fox. "I have given my life to helping your people," he said in his tired, tinny voice. "Though often I failed miserably, my intentions were always the best. Please listen to Mr. Jones and don't be so foolish as to take more of these riches than you can carry."

Red Fox's stoic countenance altered and his eyes shifted to Morning Star standing rigidly at the far end of the room. Her hand unclenched the small golden ball, and she stared transfixed at the shimmering drop.

At last Morning Star looked up at Jake. "Let us hear your ideas, Mr. Harmer," she said in a cold voice.

Jake grew uncomfortable under her unwavering glare. Shifting nervously, Jake cleared his throat and threw a desperate glance at Quinn.

"Well?" Morning Star snapped. "You don't have any ideas? You are just like the rest," she said, scorn marking each word. "All talk until you can think of a way to keep all the riches for yourself."

"No, no. I just need a private word with my bodyguard." Jake turned to Quinn. "He is also my advisor in such matters," he finished lamely.

"I think what you have to say to each other can be said to all of us," Morning Star said.

Quinn, ignoring Jake and everyone else in the room, stared at the floor and bit at the inside of his lower lip as he thought.

Save for the plink of dripping water, the silence in the room was complete.

"You have thought long enough," Morning Star said curtly. "We will hear your words. Now! Then, we will decide."

Quinn stepped into the center of the room and every eye fixed on him.

Suddenly, though, an uneasy feeling touched Ashley, a different sort of uneasiness she couldn't explain. She tried to set the feeling aside and concentrate on Mr. Jones's explanation of how he proposed to remove the gold. The feeling wouldn't be dismissed, however. Then, a slight movement like a shiver ran up Ashley's legs. A soft moan whispered through the room, and the door creaked ever so slightly. Quinn paused and glanced at the door, then began his explanation. No one else gave any sign that they noticed the creak.

Ashley, her mind guarded, her body stiff with foreboding, forced herself to appear relaxed. She leaned against the golden wall and rested her hands against the surface. The rocks were cold under her palms.

Then a gasp caught in her throat as a brief, faint tremor ran through the rock. She felt it in her hands and under her feet. There was a scrambling sound like rats scurrying over a wooden surface. Then the floor trembled, and the moan of rocks grating together shattered the quiet of the cavern.

The door jerked back and forth in erratic motion. The metal hinges, stressed into unnatural positions, grated together. Strident squeaks echoed over the grinding of the mountain. The prisoners stiffened, terrified expressions frozen on their faces.

Quinn leaped toward Red Fox. "Untie everyone's hands!" he shouted.

The mountain grated and ground together until the roar drowned out the screams of the terror-stricken people.

Indians, outlaws and passengers fled the room. As Ashley, on the far side opposite the door, tried to move, the floor under her feet tilted. In a wave-like motion, the surface rolled, crested, then sank. She slid into Quinn's outstretched arms.

"Hold on!"

He dragged her into the rolling shaft. It was a ghostly other world. All she could do was cling to Quinn and plunge unseeing through the dust-filled tunnel. Fortunately, Quinn had had the presence of mind to grab a lantern.

The tremor passed and the noise died. But the dust filled Ashley's lungs, and she coughed until she could scarcely breathe. Weak with shock and fright, she stumbled and slumped against a cold wall.

"You can't stop! The quake isn't over," Quinn shouted and pulled her forward, stumbling and running behind the others. The thunder of grinding rocks punctuated his words. Desperate, they forced their way through the narrow shaft. Suddenly, there was a sharp crack. Rocks fell from everywhere. Quinn threw himself on top of Ashley, his weight crushing her onto the floor. She slammed face first into the dirt, scarcely able to breathe. A falling rock glanced off her head, causing a shower of stars to shoot from behind her eyes. Violent bursts of pain seared through her skull.

Another resounding crash, and rocks slid down around

them from every side. Underneath, the ground tilted, stretched, and rolled wildly. Ashley clenched her fists and waited for the floor to split apart and swallow them.

The lurching, rolling motion seemed to go on endlessly. Quinn's weight on top of her grew heavier and heavier. At last, she could drag in only shallow gasps of dust laden air. She began to fade in and out of consciousness.

Dimly she heard the splinter of wood and a great roar.

Then nothing . . . .

Chapter 15

Ashley moved her eyes under closed lids, lids that seemed weighted. She struggled with all her strength against the force holding the eyelids shut. At last her efforts allowed a narrow slit of yellow light to crack the darkness.

"Well, my lady, it's good to see you awake." An unsteady voice greeted her from beyond the circle of wavering light.

Even in her semi-conscious state Ashley recognized the hollow ring of feigned cheerfulness in the voice. When she tried to question it, however, nothing came out. She ran her tongue over incredibly dry lips, but dirt clogged her mouth. In an attempt to clear her throat of the dust, she gave a dainty cough. It turned violent, and the seizure drained her tiny reservoir of strength. She had no energy left to try speaking again.

"We don't have much water yet," the voice said, "but if you had a handkerchief tucked somewhere that I could dampen and use to wipe off some of the muck . . . . "

Ashley tried to think, but her mind turned with the speed of a hibernating turtle. Where had she tucked handkerchiefs when she dressed this morning? She drew a blank. She couldn't even remember dressing this morning. In fact, she couldn't remember anything including how she came to be in this cold, damp place or who this man was.

She heard the clatter of rocks as he moved toward her. Then, without warning, he tore a strip from the bottom edge of her petticoat. The sharp ragged sound sliced into the dim silence.

"What . . . what are you doing?" she managed to croak.

"Ah . . . you can talk. That's a good sign," he said. "I was afraid maybe that last rock did more to your head than slit your scalp open."

Automatically Ashley raised a hand toward her head.

"Don't touch the cut. Let me get the dirt washed away now that the bleeding's stopped."

She watched with detachment as he dabbled the strip of petticoat in a rock-like basin of water and set about washing her face and a spot on the back of her head. His touch sent waves of fresh pain rolling through her, sickening her as it traveled. Although Ashley knew he meant her no harm, she still shrank from the hurt of his touch.

She tried to escape the pain by thinking of other things. Her thoughts, however, drifted in unconnected fragments and wouldn't focus—much like her vision. Vague pieces of scenes floated by, but the effort to hold and sort through the unrelated wisps of memory grew too great. Exhaustion won. Ashley closed her eyes and let the black velvet nothingness take her away again.

Ashley stirred and found Quinn holding her securely in his arms. Why was he taking such liberties? And why was

170

she allowing it? Pain pounded inside her head.

"Are you back to stay this time?" Quinn asked gently.

I'm not sure where I've been or where I am. She could only think her answer. Her throat was clogged and dirt sealed her mouth shut.

She blinked her eyes open again and looked up into his fatigue-lined face. His brow was furrowed with concern. She scanned the tumbled rocks and broken timbers. *What am I doing in this place?* The thought came, but the answer remained just out of reach.

"Want some water?"

She nodded and pain shot through her head.

"We don't have any food, but we have lots of water. It's been dripping a fine stream for hours. Here, open your mouth."

Opening her mouth required some time. Her tongue was too dry to help unglue her cracked lips. Quinn soaked a cloth in a small, nearby pool and dripped the water over her lips until they parted. Then, he soaked the cloth again and trickled cool water down her throat. At last the water washed away the dirt.

"I don't think anything has ever felt or tasted so good," she managed at last. "Thank you."

"How do you feel?" he asked. His concern filled the searching look he gave her.

"I'm trying very hard not to feel at all," she answered. "I hurt all over." She rested before going on. "Mr. Jones, I can't seem to remember why I'm in this terrible place. Am I dead?"

His chuckle filled the small cavern. "Cut and bruised and not functioning too well yet, but you're very much alive."

Trying to sit up, she moved out of his arms and swayed into the rock wall.

"I don't think that's such a good idea," he said and folded her to him again. "Just rest. There's no place to go and nothing to do. Sleep's the best thing for both of us."

How quickly situations change. It wasn't long ago I was nursing him and now he's doing the same for me. Her memory was coming back! At least now she could remember the past quite clearly. How she came to be in this cave with Quinn, however, still escaped her.

The effort of trying to piece together the past exhausted Ashley. The warmth of Quinn's body soothed her, and she gave herself over to the overwhelming weariness, once more drifting into untroubled sleep.

This time when Ashley woke, there was no light. She wasn't in Quinn's arms, and inky blackness hung over the cavern like a shroud. She lay in the darkness, letting her other senses take over for her eyes. Water dripped in chorus all around her, the plinks sounding with different pitches and rhythms. The dank smell of unsettled ancient earth filled her nostrils.

The earthquake! She and Quinn and—only the Lord knew how many others were trapped inside the mine.

"Mr. Jones?" she called softly, in a tenuous voice. She heard the rocks rattle next to her and felt his hand touch hers.

He cleared his throat with a rasping sound. "Good morning, sleeping beauty. Sorry the accommodations are so primitive. How do you feel?"

She felt awful, but she wasn't going to complain about her aching head and bones and hungry stomach. Not when he was trying to be so cheerful and ignore his own discomfort. "Mr. Jones, where are we?"

"Do you remember the earthquake?"

"Parts of it. Where is everyone else? Are we the only ones here?"

"Hopefully everyone else managed to get out before things fell in. This is a small cave in the debris from the collapse of the mine shaft. We were fortunate to have been

172

in the right place at the right time."

A slow death by starvation could hardly be called "fortunate," she thought. The full impact of their situation was beginning to register with Ashley. There was no way to know if any of the others got out of the mine alive. And if they had, nobody would think she and Mr. Jones were still alive, trapped deep inside the mountain.

The thought that they weren't going to get out of this finally rooted, and Ashley's stomach reeled.

She began to shake uncontrollably. If she didn't get her mind off their predicament, she was going to become hysterical and turn into a screaming, sobbing heap in front of Mr. Jones.

Drawing several deep breaths, Ashley calmed herself. At least she wasn't going to have to worry about marrying. Lord Peter would become the sole heir to her mother's money and never have to live in the poverty he so feared. She closed her eyes again and tried to drive away the depressing thoughts. She found herself quoting Psalm 23. Gradually she relaxed.

"That's the way," Mr. Jones said gently, smoothing her hair away from her forehead. "Go back to sleep. Best possible healer for your hurts."

The temptation to sleep was great, but if these were the last hours she had left on earth, she didn't want to sleep them away.

"Tell me, Mr. Jones," Ashley began in a trembling voice, "how did you discover gold in so remote a place as this?"

Quinn glanced at her, lifted an eyebrow in surprise, then chuckled. "Well, Jake and I had an old mule named Sally," he began. The words came out slowly as though he was savoring each one before releasing it. "She'd been with us through high times and low. We were in a bad low a few years back, and about ready to give it all up. We camped for the night in that saddle in the mountain above the mine entrance and spent a good amount of time discussing our plight. We hobbled Sally and she started to graze down the steep slope. Got part-way down the mountain and refused to climb back up when we were ready to move on the next morning. When Jake hiked down to get her, he thought the rock looked promising. The Sally Forth mine is the result."

"You named the mine after the mule?" Ashley asked.

"If it hadn't been for her sallying forth, we'd have gone right on by. God had to be guiding us. When we drove the shaft, we found the vein of ore runs horizontal and that makes things much easier. Back here in these hills, we could never have gotten big engines in to haul the ore out of a vertical shaft. We ran the shaft in under the vein, dynamited the ore, and let it fall down of its own weight. We've taken out a king's ransom and still haven't come close to exhausting what's here."

Why did Ashley have the feeling Quinn owned the mine? Though he used the term 'we,' the lilt in his voice as he talked, and his sense of possession gave her the feeling Jake had very little to do with running the mine.

"We get mostly gold from the Sally Forth, with some silver, zinc, and trash metals mixed in."

"Do you own all of the mountain?"

"No, only some of it. I . . we'd been working this claim for quite some time before anybody heard about it and took claims around us."

"You mean you don't own the land around the Sally Forth?"

"No, but this is the major vein in the district. Nobody else's claims ever amounted to much, and they just gave up and moved on."

"But if you don't own the claims next to the Sally Forth, what do you do if your vein runs onto someone else's claim?"

"Good question," he said in a surprised voice. "Law says I can follow my vein wherever it leads, regardless of who has the surface rights. I can't go *onto* another man's claim, but I can mine *under* it as far as my ore runs."

Ashley noticed he had slipped into claiming the mine. *Interesting!* "Do you have any other claims besides this one?"

"Took the precaution of filing on several others just in case this one peters out."

"Mr. Jones, it is my distinct impression that *you* are the owner of the mine, not Mr. Harmer."

There was a long silence. "I don't suppose it will hurt to tell you," he said at last. "Sally and I found and claimed all these mines. When they showed such rich color, I knew I would be besieged for my wealth by everyone and anyone. I have no longing for that kind of notoriety. Jake came along early on, an old prospector down on his luck. Dressed up, he looked the part of a rich mine owner. He liked the show of riches and by pretending to be his bodyguard, I stayed close to all the business. Worked fine for both of us."

"That certainly does explain a great many things about you."

"I'm curious," Quinn said, changing the subject. "What is a beautiful English lady doing traveling in this wild country?"

"Accompanying my father on his travels," she answered. "He loves people and is forever curious about anyone or any place he hasn't seen." Ashley still wasn't ready to talk about her real reason, and she changed the subject. "Do you have family other than Davey here?"

He didn't answer at once. Finally he cleared his throat, but a tightness showed that hadn't been there before. "Davey's not family. Not in the way you mean."

"He's not your son?"

"Not really. I found him and Hiller wandering in the hills a few years back. Couldn't talk, didn't seem to hear. Just a blank. Got him so he responds to hugging, and his eyes light up if something especially pleases him. He finally

175

smiled last Christmas and this year at his birthday party."

"How do you know when his birthday is?"

"We don't. Just made up a day and celebrate it. Every kid needs a birthday."

"I don't mean to intrude, but you are an attractive man with much to offer a wife and family. Why is it you have never married?"

"I've been traipsing through this country for a lot of years. Seen what it does to women. Turns them old before their time, sours their dispositions. With precious little medical help, many die in childbirth, leaving helpless infants to be raised by grieving fathers. Davey is a prime example of what this country does to families. I swore I'd never bring a woman I loved here until I was willing to leave if she wanted. I've tried going away, but something always drags me back. Something inside me can't live without the strength the mountains impart."

His reasons weren't what Ashley wanted to hear. Then she caught herself. In their present circumstance, his unwillingness to marry didn't matter.

She stared unseeingly into the blackness. A picture of her childhood home rose in her mind. The lovely old house was so full of beauty and warmth; it was a house she loved with all her heart.

Ashley imagined herself riding her horse on the moors in the brisk clean air of October, and then quite unexpectedly she saw Quinn Jones' face. He sat a fine black gelding, and he rode toward her from the opposite direction, a smile of anticipation lighting his face.

She closed her eyes and her heart clenched, producing an aching throb in her chest. She must not think of him. It was a useless dream. He had already said he would never marry until he could bring himself to leave the mountains. Besides, even believing as she did that the Lord could do anything, it didn't look like they were going to get out of this alive.

"Tell me about yourself, Lady Ashley," he said, breaking the heavy silence.

"What makes you think I'm titled?"

"I was born in England and spent the first ten years of my life there. Young as I was, I haven't forgotten that much. Besides, now that touring America is fashionable, we see the gentry frequently in and about Denver."

"How did you get to America?"

"My father heard how easy it was to become rich. 'Just pick up giant nuggets off the ground,' he was told. He sold everything and off he sailed, my mother and me his unwilling followers. We suffered the trip west and all the indignities imaginable while he struggled to find a rich vein. While he rushed from dig to dig, I stayed in Virginia City with mother and learned everything I could about hard-rock mining.

"Finally, the country and the hard life broke my poor mother. She died up in Montana after we followed my father to another big strike. She saw to it I had schooling and a Christian upbringing, even under impossible circumstances. A truly remarkable woman, my mother."

At the sound of love in his voice, Ashley's heart plummeted. "And ever since, you have compared every woman you met with her. We all fall too far short to be acceptable."

When Quinn failed to respond to her comment, Ashley knew she had hit the mark.

After an uncomfortable pause, Ashley asked, "What happened to your father?"

"When he came back from the hills and found my mother gone, he drifted away. I have no idea where he went. I never saw him again. I was seventeen, big as an elephant and strong as an ox. I had no trouble finding work, and when people learned I could read and do sums, I didn't have to work in the mines to make a good living." He paused. "The rest you know. Now, it's your turn, Ashley.

177

You keep changing the subject when we talk about your life."

"You're right. I have avoided my story because there are parts I'm not proud of. Now, however, it's not going to matter what you think of me."

Since there was no hope of being rescued and nothing else to occupy the remaining hours of their lives, she spun the story to the limit, leaving out no details.

When she was finished, Quinn began his story. However, it had been two days since the earthquake. Sometime during Quinn's first successful gold strike in Nevada, Ashley drifted into unconsciousness.

Chapter 16

Ashley strained against the weight on her eyelids and fought to open her eyes.

"I do believe she's coming round," Lord Peter's voice boomed.

"Land sakes, I hope so," Molly said. "Child's been unconscious for nearly a week. Began to think she'd never make it."

"Somebody go stop Quinn," Jake ordered. "Boy doesn't need to make the ride for a doctor. Never would have made it to Durango anyway. Not with the road over the mountain blocked by snow and the sky looking to dump more today."

Ashley felt a spoon on her lips and eagerly sipped at the contents.

"That's right, lamb. You take all the broth you want. Molly's chicken soup'll fix you up in no time."

Molly spooned warm soup into Ashley's mouth. "Not so fast, child, you'll choke. I know you're starved, but you'll

179

have to eat slow at first."

Ashley gave up trying to open her eyes. When her stomach felt warm and satisfied, she drifted into a deep sleep.

In contented reverie, Ashley let her eyes travel lazily around the room until they rested on a picture of cheerful daisies hanging beside the door. It was a calendar! The sight jarred her. Her heart raced. What was the date? Had her birthday come and gone? Ashley tried to count the days, but she couldn't. She had no idea how long she and Quinn had been sealed inside the mountain, or how long it had been since their rescue.

If her birthday hadn't come and gone, Lord Peter was undoubtedly down in Harmer City attempting to locate a man who would agree to become her husband.

Ashley shuddered. She had seen the rough, hard-living men who dug for gold in the Nevada mining camps. In its design, Harmer City differed little from those other camps.

Molly was a good example of the women who followed their men into the mining towns—kind of heart, but as unrefined as the raw ore their husbands mined. It took that kind of toughness to survive in these places.

Dear Lord, why didn't you let me die in that earthquake? Father would have his money, and I would be saved from this awful fate. Help me to trust you more, Lord. I haven't done very well at it lately. Forgive me.

The complications of her situation overwhelmed Ashley, and her lower lip began trembling. Though she clenched her jaws and bit the offending lip, nothing stopped the flow of tears. At last, she gave in and sobbed out her anger and frustration.

A knock roused Ashley. Wiping furiously at the tears with the back of her hand, she looked at the washstand. But when she tried to move to wash away the tear streaks, she grew dizzy. With heart pounding and knees trembling, she sank back into the pillows.

Another knock. "Come in," she called in a weak voice.

The door burst open, and Ashley stared at Molly. The flowered figure, smiling a gap-toothed smile, sailed into the room and over to Ashley's bedside.

"Ya look mighty elegant today. Now if I do say so, ya need to use your charms on Quinn."

"Molly!" Ashley gasped, blushing to her hair roots. Trying to change the subject, she asked, "What is today's date?"

Molly rolled on, ignoring Ashley's question. "He needs a wife, and that little waif needs a mother. From what I've seen, you'd work out just fine in both jobs."

Ashley wanted to slide through a crack in the floor. "Mr. Jones has made it very plain that he doesn't want a permanent attachment to any woman."

"That's the story he sticks to, but I don't believe it. If he didn't want a home life, why'd he pick up Davey and bring him here? Could just as well have dropped him off at an orphanage in Denver. Nope. I don't believe for one minute he don't want a wife. But he ain't gonna give up his freedom without a fight." Molly shook a finger in Ashley's face. "Ya want this man, ya gotta make him feel strong and manly." Giving Ashley's hair a pat, Molly hurried to the door. "I gotta get back down to the kitchen and finish supper. You stay right there, lyin' on them pillows like ya are. Good to see ya awake at last. I'll tell Quinn ya wanta see him."

"No!" Ashley protested, but Molly had already slammed the door shut and was pounding her way downstairs.

Ashley felt sick with humiliation. Lord Peter was out trying to buy her a husband, and now Molly was going to send Quinn upstairs so Ashley could persuade him to marry her. Why, oh, why, hadn't she died in that earthquake! She struggled out of bed. A wave of nausea swept over her; she staggered and collapsed on the floor.

The sun was streaming through the unshuttered window when Ashley blinked awake again. Quinn stirred in the rocker, stretched with lithe grace, and sat up.

"Mr. Jones, what day is it?" Ashley asked, dreading the answer.

At the sound of her voice, he leaped to his feet. "Ashley!" he cried and knelt beside the bed. "Thank God you're back with us. How do you feel?" Gently he stroked her hair. "We've been holding a prayer vigil, but you've been unconscious for so many days, even your father and I were ready to give up."

Ashley gave a weak cry. "Days! How many days? When did they find us?"

Quinn pursed his lips and thoughts. "It's been about ten days, I'd say. I still have some difficulty remembering everything clearly. They dug us out just a few hours after you became unconscious."

"Never mind. Tell me the date," she demanded.

"Well, I'll have to look on the calendar. Is knowing the exact date important?"

"It is exceedingly important."

"Very well, then." With considerable reluctance, Quinn pushed himself to his feet and strolled over to the calendar.

"It's the first day of November," he announced.

"November! It can't be November," Ashley wailed.

"It is, Ashley. It most definitely is."

Lord Peter entered the room, and she turned stricken eyes to him. "Oh, Father, whatever shall we do? I've let you down!" Heartsick, Ashley unsuccessfully fought the tears streaming in uncontrolled rivers.

"Here, here," Lord Peter clucked. "No need to be so emotional. What's done is done. Can't bring back the past, you know. Your birthday is tomorrow. Right now—now, I'm thankful to have you alive. We'll just have to live with what we have."

"Father, we don't *have* anything. How are you going to

live on it?" Ashley struggled to sit up. This didn't sound like the father she knew—the one who was willing to marry her to anyone.

"Ashley, you stay right where you are," Quinn ordered. "If you get any more upset, your father's going to have to leave without telling you goodbye."

Ashley collapsed back against the pillows, not so much because of Quinn's order but because her head spun with sickening intensity. "What do you mean, tell Father goodbye?" she croaked through a dry throat.

"Ashley, my dear, you told me about that wretched will, and Lord Peter has filled in the details," Quinn said gently. "You have all my sympathy. The prospect of having to marry someone you didn't love and who didn't love you is unthinkable."

"But Quinn and I have everything worked out," Lord Peter interrupted. "There's a break in the weather this morning. With Riley as our guide on the trail I'm taking Morton Sterling and leaving immediately for Denver and then on to England. I'm to be the representative for the Sally Forth in London and Sterling will be my financial advisor. We're going to sell stock in the findings here. With my British contacts and his investment knowledge, we'll all grow rich." Lord Peter glowed.

"Your beautiful home in England is saved," she whispered. "Thank you, Lord." The years of struggling to honor her father were rewarded—and she hadn't had to marry a man who didn't know the Lord!

The jangling of spurs drew their attention to Riley striding through the doorway. "Lord Peter, if we're gonna make Durango today, we're gonna have t' get a move on," he said. "Will's waitin' downstairs with the burros."

A flurry of farewells sent Lord Peter and Morton Sterling on their way. Ashley listened as the house grew quiet. She could hear the last goodbyes echoing through the thin air, and her heart caught in her throat. What was going to become of her?

Exhausted by the sudden and emotional farewell, Ashley couldn't think clearly. She allowed her eyes to close and she drifted once more into sleep.

A knock, rapid and demanding, startled Ashley awake. "Yes?" she called.

"Are you feeling up to visitors?" Quinn asked from the hall.

Her hand flew to her hair. She must look a sight.

"I promise not to stay long, but I would like to see how you're doing," he called.

Then, without waiting for Ashley's permission, he opened the door. He looked wonderful standing there, so like when she first bumped into him in Durango. The cold lump in her heart melted at the sight of him.

"C...c...come in. And sit down." Automatically, she motioned to a chair.

He relaxed into the rocker beside her bed as though he planned a long stay. Rocking in silence, his eyes remained fixed on her face.

"I haven't thanked you for saving my life," she said at last. "I should never have gotten out alive if you hadn't nursed me so well. Did everyone escape the mine?"

He looked slightly uneasy. "Morning Star and all her warriors have gone back to the tribe. Alive but, unfortunately, without the riches they dreamed of."

"And Pastor Grove?"

"Had a bit more stress than he could handle. He's still recovering. He wants to remain here in Harmer City. Come spring we're going to start building him a church." Quinn studied her carefully. "Sidell and Litch are dead."

"They were evil men, but I am sorry nevertheless." Ashley lowered her eyes. "I think I remember telling you ... everything ... about ... about .... "

Quinn nodded. "Everything."

She turned away, her face ashen.

She could hear Quinn squirm on the slick surface of the

chair. The clock, with its measured ticking, filled the awkward silence. At last, he said, "Lord Peter told me you have refused all the eligible men he arranged for you to meet. No one lives up to your exacting standards."

"As you know, without the pressure of Mother's will, they did not think I would ever marry. Father wants Mother's money to keep the estate and an heir to carry on the Ferguson line."

"I think he's more anxious for that heir. Money can't buy him a grandchild."

"Did Father also tell you that the man I married must be willing to change his name to Ferguson so the child would carry that name?"

"Yes, he told me," Quinn said, studying her face intently. Their eyes met and she found his unreadable.

He started to stand and Ashley, before she even thought, reached out and laid a hand on his arm.

Quinn laid his hand on hers, pinning her to him. She tried not to notice the coldness of his hand or to think about the strength in the fingers that gently stroked her wrist.

Quinn raised his eyes and now she could see golden flecks swimming in the green depths.

"What are you trying to say to me?" she asked.

He took a deep breath and licked his lips. "I love you. I want to marry you . . . to make you my wife for real this time. But I only want you if you love me, too."

"Oh, Mr. Jones," Ashley breathed, "I've loved you ever since you saved me from that horrible bandit by saying I was your wife."

"That isn't love you feel. That's gratitude."

"That's a form of love, and it certainly wasn't a bad base to start from. And I promise you, what I feel isn't gratitude. But there's one question more important than all the others that I must ask you." Hesitating a little, Ashley drew a deep breath, then said, "I accepted Christ as my personal Saviour when I was twelve. He means everything to me—even though I haven't always shown it recently. That is the main reason Father and I have traveled all over the world. I could only share my life with a man who also loved the Lord."

A wondrous light flooded Quinn's face as he interrupted her.

"Just before we left London, when I was a lad of nine, we went regularly to the services in the New Park Street Chapel. I accepted Christ that year under Mr. Spurgeon's preaching. I must admit," he said somewhat reluctantly, "I haven't always done right, but I do love my Lord and try to serve Him every day of my life."

Joy filled Ashley's heart as she said, "I knew. In my heart I've felt that you must be a Christian, too. You've shown your Christian kindness in so many ways." Her lips curved into a teasing smile. "Have you repented of your impulsive falsehoods?"

He smiled. "I have."

"Then, I could learn to love you, Mr. Jones, but it would take a very long time. A lifetime, at least."

"My dearest Ashley, would you really consider becoming my wife?"

"I would be most honored to accept your proposal. Provided, of course, you don't wish a long engagement."

He knelt beside the bed and took her in his arms. "That could pose a problem," he said solemnly. "I had always dreamed of being engaged at least twelve hours. Is that too long?"

Ashley slipped her arms around his shoulders and laughed. "That's just about right, Mr. Jones," she whispered.

"We do have another problem. I can't have you going around calling me 'Mr. Jones.' Name's Quinn."

Ashley's face fell. In her joy at becoming Quinn's wife, she had forgotten about the name!

His eyes widened and grew dark green. "What's the matter, now?"

"I . . I forgot about the name. You know . . . changing your name to Ferguson. I would still like to do that for Father."

Quinn gave a relieved laugh. "That's not a problem. I've never been particularly attached to Jones. How would you feel about a hyphenated version, Ferguson-Jones? Certainly lends distinction to 'Jones'."

"Oh, Quinn," she breathed, "if you don't mind it, I think the name is wonderful."

Ashley rested her head in the hollow of his shoulder. For a few moments they were quiet, then Quinn said, "Ashley, I want you to know . . . about the mine . . . I've seen many a man who thought he had married a fine loving woman, then learned that all the lady wanted was his money. When the woman had bankrupted the poor sucker, she left him broken in spirit and bank account. I guess I didn't trust the Lord enough to give me a good Christian woman who loved me for me, so I persuaded Jake to play the rich mine owner. He has enjoyed it greatly, but it was wrong. I've asked the Lord to forgive me and wanted you to know, too."

"But how have you lived a lie and felt comfortable with God?"

"It hasn't been comfortable. I'm glad it's over and the truth is out. However, I don't plan any more deceptions—even for the sake of a lovely woman."

She laughed and Quinn joined her.

"Isn't this wonderful? We were both searching for the same things. Oh, Quinn, the Lord is truly great if we will but trust in Him."

"Yes, He is, dear Ashley. Yes, He is."

Their lips met while their love soared, spiraling upward and healing all their wounds.

At last, in a husky voice, he said, "Let me find Davey. He'll be one happy boy to learn you're going to stay on as his mother."

Ashley released Quinn and folded her hands in her lap.

"I wish Father knew," she said wistfully.

"I have a feeling he does, my dearest." And Quinn kissed her once more.

Historical Footnote

In 1914, a vug such as is used in this story, was actually discovered. The Cresson Mine in Cripple Creek, Colorado was the site of a treasure of unbelievable richness—and rarity.

By this time the easy placers were depleted and miners were digging far down into hard rock, following veins that ran hundreds, even thousands, of feet below the surface. At the 1,200 foot level of the Cresson Mine, a crew under the direction of Dick Roelofs cut through hard rock into a cavity. Technically called a geode, it was commonly called a vug in miner's slang.

When Dick and his crew cut into this opening, he used the light from his miner's hat to look through the small hole into the room. One look and Roelofs knew he had never seen anything to compare with it. He immediately sent for an ironworker to build a vault door and posted armed guards.

He also sent for two honorable, trusted men before entering the room himself. When they did, they stepped into a wonderland of solid gold. The vug was 20 feet long, 15 feet wide, and 40 feet high. The walls glittered with pure gold crystals and 24 carat flakes. Some were as big as a man's thumbnail. Pure gold boulders littered the floor.

The most trusted miners scraped the walls and filled 1,400 sacks with crystals and flakes, 1,000 sacks of lower grade ore, and mined the outer layers of rock. The vug was stripped in four weeks and netted $1,200,000.